PAWS

MINDY MAKES SOME SPACE

MICHELE ASSARASAKORN
NATHAN FAIRBAIRN

RAZORBILL

RAZORBILL

An imprint of Penguin Random House LLC, New York

First published in the United States of America by Razorbill,
an imprint of Penguin Random House LLC, 2022

Visit us online at penguinrandomhouse.com.

Library of Congress Cataloging-in-Publication Data is available.
ISBN 9780593351932 (paperback)
1 3 5 7 9 10 8 6 4 2
ISBN 9780593351918 (hardcover)
1 3 5 7 9 10 8 6 4 2

Book manufactured in Canada

TC

Illustrated by Michele Assarasakorn
Written, colored, and lettered by Nathan Fairbairn

Edited by Christopher Hernandez
Design by Maria Fazio

Text set in CCJoeKubert

We acknowledge the support of the Canada Council for the Arts.

For Peggy.
Thanks for everything, Mom.
You are so loved.

—N. F.

For Kiki.

—M. A.

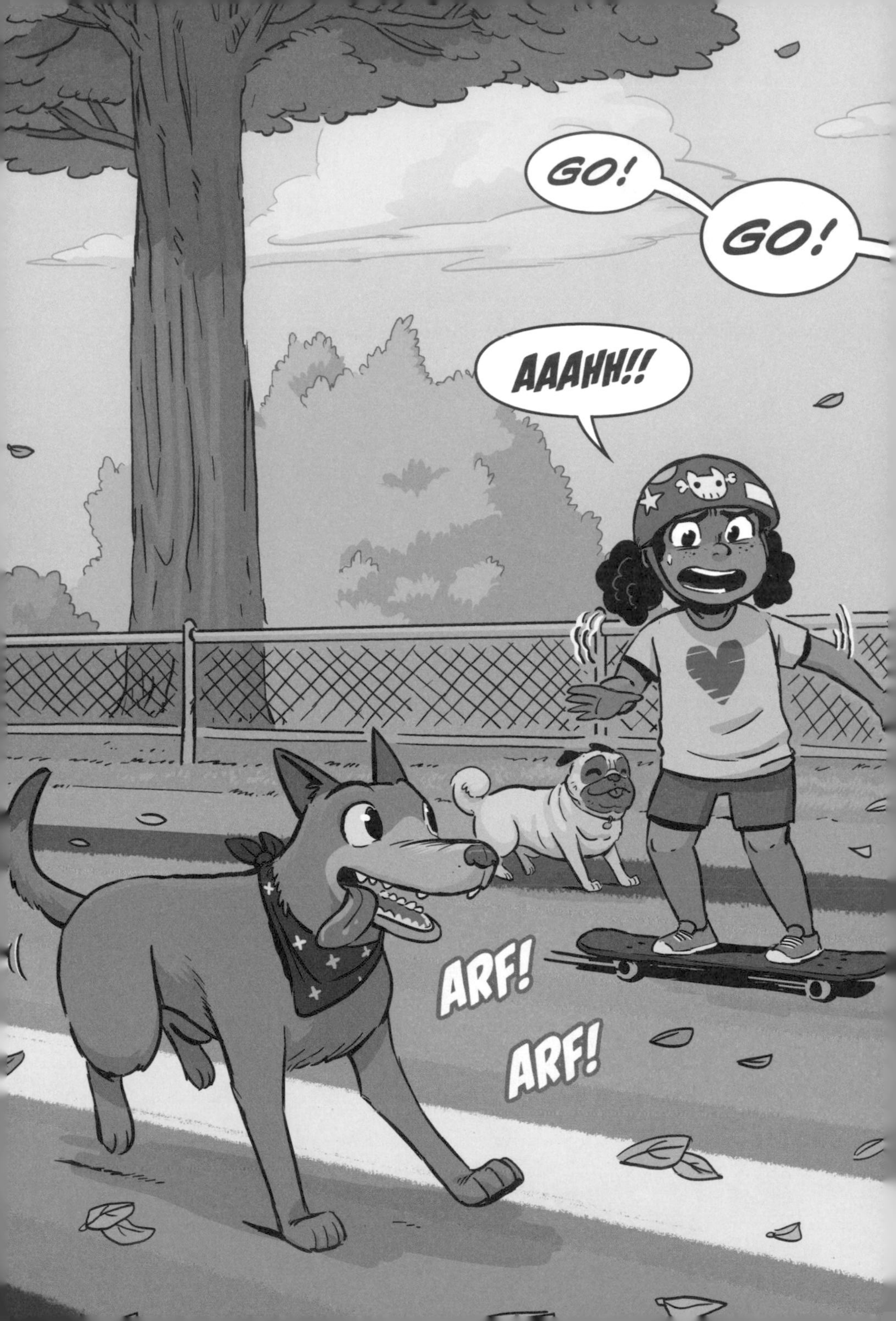
GO!
GO!
AAAHH!!
ARF!
ARF!

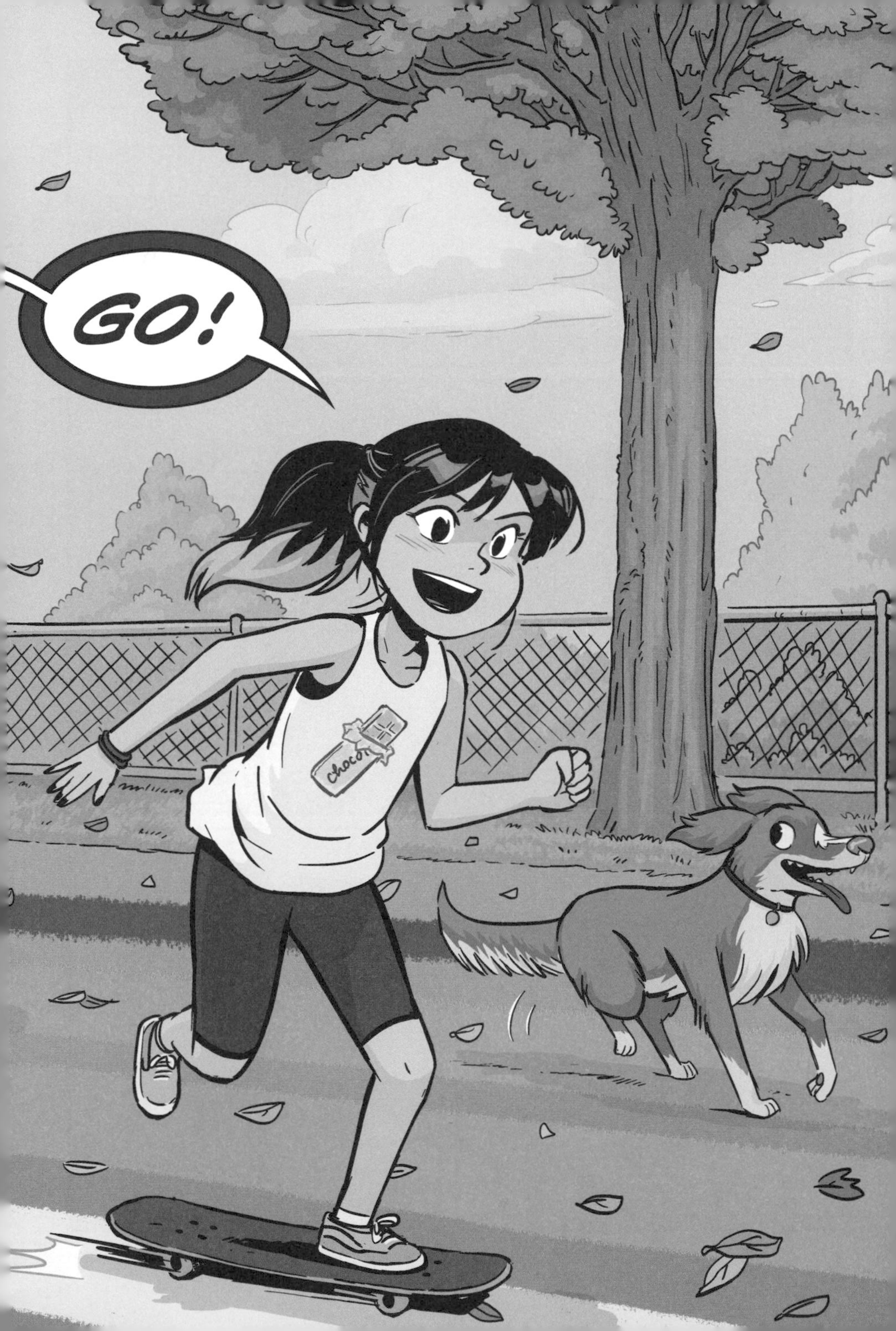
GO!
choco

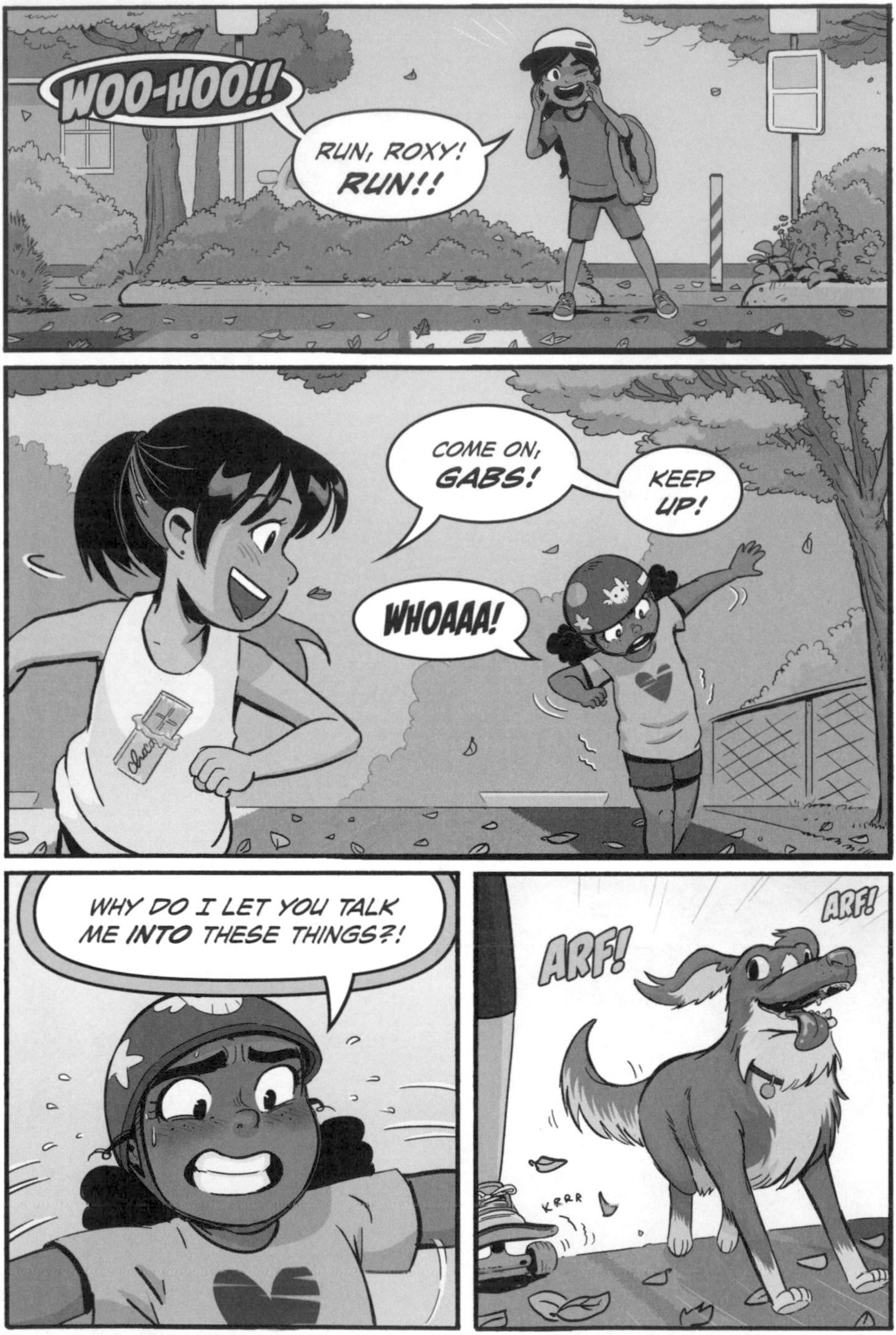
WOO-HOO!!
RUN, ROXY! RUN!!
COME ON, GABS!
KEEP UP!
WHOAAA!
WHY DO I LET YOU TALK ME INTO THESE THINGS?!
ARF!
ARF!

ROXY **WINS!**

ARF!

ARF!!

GOOD GIRL!! **GOOD GIRL!!**

AWWWW...

I THOUGHT I **HAD** HER THIS TIME!

AH, WELL! GOOD RACE, EVERYONE!

EVEN YOU, GABBY! I THINK YOU'RE GETTING A LOT...

AAAAHH!

...BETTER?

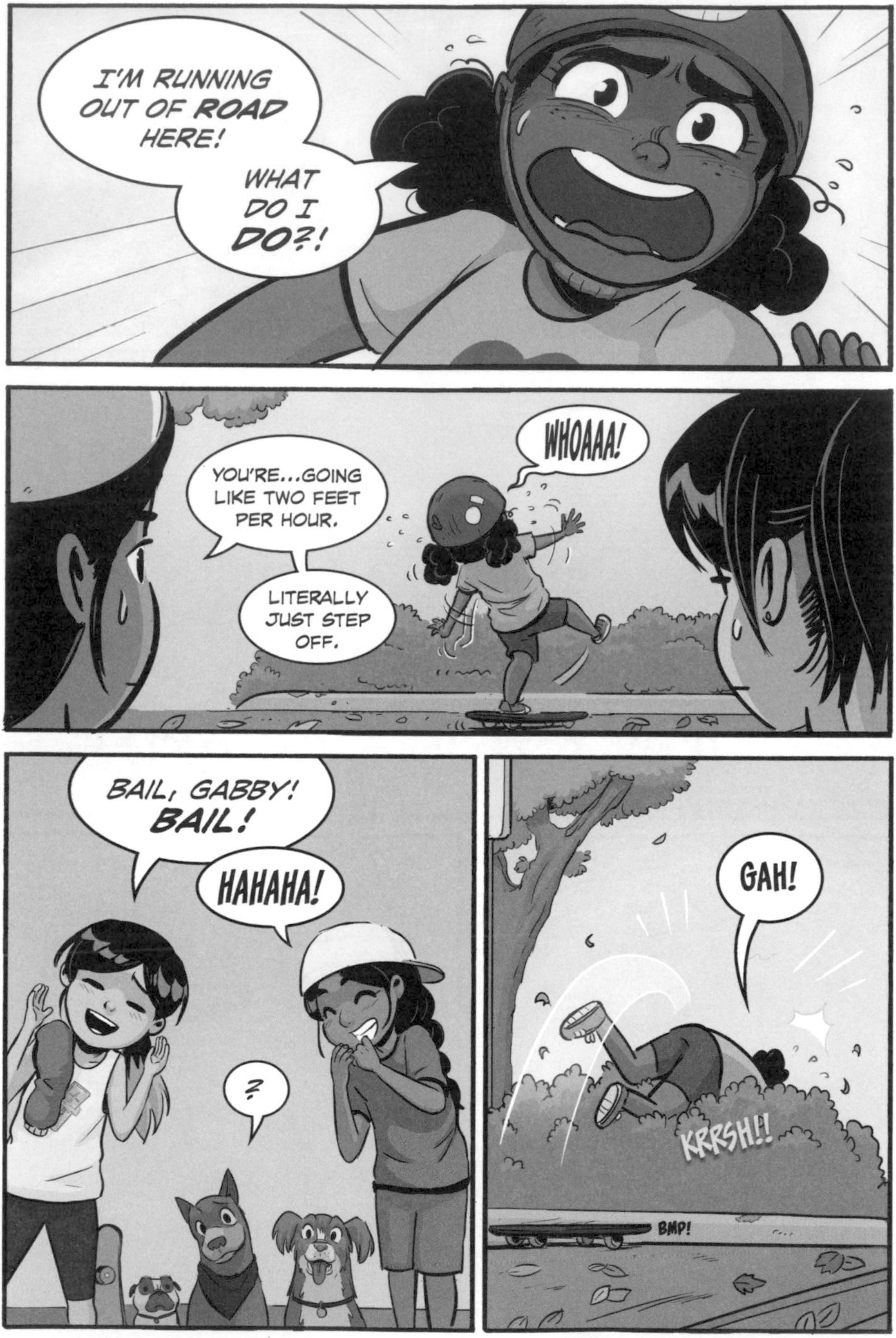
I'M RUNNING OUT OF ROAD HERE!
WHAT DO I DO?!
YOU'RE...GOING LIKE TWO FEET PER HOUR.
LITERALLY JUST STEP OFF.
WHOAAA!
BAIL, GABBY! BAIL!
HAHAHA!
?
GAH!
KRRSH!!
BMP!

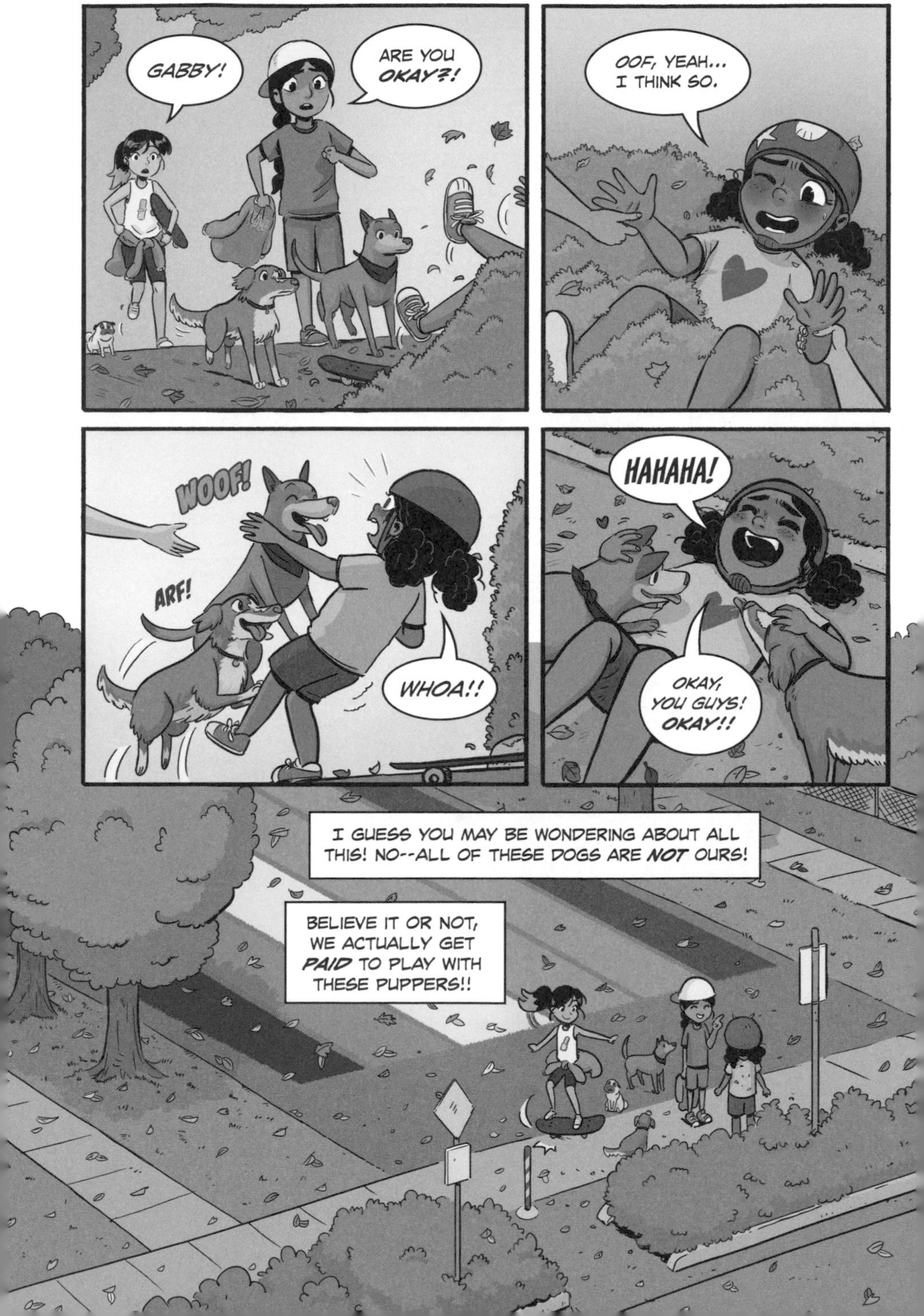
GABBY!
ARE YOU OKAY?!
OOF, YEAH... I THINK SO.
WOOF!
ARF!
WHOA!!
HAHAHA!
OKAY, YOU GUYS! OKAY!!
I GUESS YOU MAY BE WONDERING ABOUT ALL THIS! NO--ALL OF THESE DOGS ARE NOT OURS!
BELIEVE IT OR NOT, WE ACTUALLY GET PAID TO PLAY WITH THESE PUPPERS!!

MY NAME IS MINDY PARK, AND THESE ARE MY TWO **BEST** BUDS IN THE WHOLE WORLD--

GABBY JORDAN AND PRIYA GUPTA!

YOU MIGHT THINK WE'RE A BIT OF AN **ODD SQUAD,** UNTIL YOU REALLY GET TO KNOW US.

LIKE, PRIYA CAN BE **SO** SWEET, BUT SHE'S ALSO GOT A **TOTAL** COMPETITIVE SIDE.

SHE PLAYS JUST ABOUT **EVERY** SPORT...

...AND SHE'S GREAT AT THEM **ALL!**

GABBY, ON THE OTHER HAND, ISN'T EXACTLY THE SPORTY TYPE, TO PUT IT **MILDLY.** SHE'S NOT GONNA WIN ANY RACES, UNLESS THEY HAVE SPEED **READING** RACES.

(WAIT, **DO** THEY HAVE THOSE? I BET THEY DO. PEOPLE ARE SO WEIRD.)

Old Dutch

PERSONALLY, I DON'T **DO** SPORTS, UNLESS YOU COUNT SKATEBOARDING.

AND I'M REALLY NOT A BIG FAN OF READING, UNLESS IT'S GRAPHIC NOVELS OR MANGA. **THOSE** I LIKE!

I ALSO LIKE TO LOOK FOR COOL CLOTHES AT THRIFT SHOPS, EAT JUNK FOOD, AND LOOK AT MY PHONE.

LOL--SOMETIMES I EVEN DO ALL THREE AT THE SAME TIME. THAT'S LIVING THE **DREAM!**

GABBY'S A GRADE BEHIND ME AND PRIYA, BUT WE'RE ALL IN THE SAME CLASS. OUR SCHOOL--*CHARLOTTE BRÖNTE ELEMENTARY*--IS ALL ABOUT THE COMBINED CLASSES.

ANYWAY, WE'RE PRETTY DIFFERENT PEOPLE, BUT ONE THING WE SHARE IS THAT *WE'RE ALL COMPLETELY WILD ABOUT ANIMALS!*

AND WHAT **REALLY** BROUGHT US TOGETHER WAS THAT, WHEN WE FIRST STARTED HANGING OUT, NONE OF US COULD GET OUR HANDS ON *ANY.*

SEE, GABBY'S DAD IS A TOTAL NEAT FREAK WHO DOESN'T LIKE ANIMALS...

PRIYA'S MOM HAS BAD ALLERGIES...

AND MY MOM AND I LIVE IN A PLACE THAT DOESN'T *ALLOW* ANIMALS.

IT'S A *MAJOR* BUMMER.

VACANCY
1 BEDROOM
NO PETS ALLOWED

AH-CHOO!

AH!

VRMMMM

SO A LITTLE WHILE AGO WE CAME UP WITH A PLAN TO GET OUR HANDS ON SOME *FLOOFS!*

THE PLAN:
1. MAKE FRIENDS WITH SOMEONE WITH A CAT?
2. ANIMAL RESCUE.
3. VOLUNTEER AT SPCA TO WALK DOGS.
4. VOLUNTEER AT A VETERINARY CLINIC.

THE PLAN DIDN'T QUITE WORK OUT *EXAAAAAACTLY* AS, UM, PLANNED...

...BUT IT *DID* WORK!!

THE VANCOUVER VETERINARY HOSPITAL

WE ENDED UP STARTING A DOG WALKING BUSINESS CALLED *PAWS*, WHICH STANDS FOR *PRETTY AWESOME WALKERS*.

(SWEET NAME, RIGHT?! *I* CAME UP WITH IT!)

WE GOT OFF TO A ROUGH START, AND FOR A WHILE IT LOOKED LIKE THE WHOLE THING WAS GOING TO FALL APART.

BUT WE PULLED IT TOGETHER IN THE END! AND NOW THINGS ARE GOING *GREAT!*

WE HAVE *FIVE* DOGS, WHO EACH GET WALKED TWO OR THREE TIMES A WEEK--

SCRAPS

PICKLES

ROXY

CARL

CORPORAL WAGS

IT'S ABSOLUTELY *PERFECT!* I HOPE IT NEVER *EVER* CHANGES!

9

THANKS FOR LETTING ME TRY YOUR OLD BOARD, MINDY...

BUT I THINK I'LL JUST STICK TO MY FEET NEXT TIME.

HA! DON'T GIVE UP NOW! THAT WAS YOUR BEST RIDE *YET!*

FORGET IT--THAT IS THE *LAST* TIME I GET ON A MODE OF TRANSPORTATION THAT DOESN'T HAVE THE SENSE TO USE *BRAKES!*

HAHA--THEY DON'T *NEED* BRAKES! DO *ROLLER SKATES* HAVE BRAKES?

OKAY, MY AUNTIE SHATTERED HER *WRIST* LAST YEAR ON ROLLER SKATES, SO THAT IS *NOT* A WINNING ARGUMENT.

OMG, GABBY. YOU'RE SO...SO...

SO *WHAT??*

CAREFUL!!

YOU SAY THAT LIKE IT'S A *BAD* THING!

HAHA...COME ON, GUYS. CUT IT OUT.

OH! I ALMOST *FORGOT!* MOM SAID I COULD INVITE YOU GUYS OVER FOR DINNER. SHE'S MAKING YOUR *FAVORITE,* GABBY--ALOO GOBI!

OH, YUM! WILL THERE BE GARLIC NAAN?

OF *COURSE!*

COUNT ME *IN!*

SOUNDS GREAT, PRIYA-- BUT MY MOM AND I ARE HAVING A GIRLS' NIGHT AND I'VE BEEN LOOKING FORWARD TO IT ALL *WEEK.*

AHH, TOO *BAD.* I GUESS THAT JUST MEANS MORE FOR US! I CALL DIBS ON MINDY'S GULAB JAMUN!

HAHA!

?

DREAM *ON,* GABS! IF ANY SWEETS ARE LEFT OVER, THOSE BABIES ARE ALLLLL MINE!

SNIFF!

SNIFF!

HEY, CARL! WHATCHA SNIFFING DOWN THERE, BUDD--

SNIFF!

SNIFF!

GULP!

AAAAAAHHH!

WHAT WAS THAT?!

WHAT DID YOU JUST EA--

SLURP!

ACK! RIGHT ON MY MOUTH!

PFT!

DID ANYONE SEE WHAT IT *WAS*??

ALL I SAW WAS THAT IT WAS BROWN AND LUMPY!

SO...EITHER CHOCOLATE OR...POO?

OH, MAN...I HOPE IT WAS POO.

WHAT?!

WELL, *THINK* ABOUT IT! CHOCOLATE IS *POISONOUS* TO DOGS!!

TK TK TK

YEAH, B-BUT...BUT ...POO.

I KNOW!

ON MY MOUTH.

I KNOW!!

GUYS! THIS SITE SAYS EVEN IF IT *WAS* A BIT OF CHOCOLATE BAR--

WHICH, YUCK, IT PROBABLY WASN'T--

A DOG CARL'S SIZE WOULD HAVE TO EAT *WAY* MORE TO GET SICK!

PHEW! STILL, WE SHOULD TELL HIS OWNER TO KEEP AN EYE ON HIM.

UGH...CARL, WHYYY???

MMFFF!

WHAT?

"I HOPE IT WAS POO."

HAHAHAHAHA!

13

LATER...

MOM! I'M *HOME!*

OMG, WAIT TILL YOU HEAR ABOUT WHAT *CARL* DID ON THE WALK TODAY!!

ONE SEC, HON! JUST FINISHING UP SOMETHING IMPORTANT!

OH, YEAH, R//////GHT...

THIS IS MY MOM! HER NAME IS SUN HEE, BUT MOST PEOPLE JUST CALL HER *SUNNY.* SHE'S THE *BEST!*

CLICK CLICK CLICK CLICK

SHE PLAYS A LOT OF VIDEO GAMES. THEY'RE NOT REALLY MY THING, BUT SHE'S *REALLY* GOOD AT THEM. ESPECIALLY THIS *ONE* GAME...

HORDE OF HEROES AGAIN?

YEP, WE ARE WINNING *SO HARD!*

HORDE OF HEROES IS THIS ONLINE THING WHERE YOU PLAY WITH A TEAM? I THINK YOU'RE A BUNCH OF SUPERHEROES WHO FIGHT A BUNCH OF BAD GUYS?

...COME AND...GET IT...

ANYWAY, IT'S PRETTY POPULAR. MOST OF THE BOYS IN MY CLASS PLAY IT. I THINK THEY LIKE IT BECAUSE THEY CAN ALL PLAY TOGETHER WITHOUT EVER LEAVING THEIR **HOUSES.**

MOM DOESN'T REALLY KNOW **ANY** OF THE PEOPLE SHE PLAYS WITH, THOUGH. WHICH IS KIND OF A BUMMER. I SOMETIMES THINK I SHOULD GET INTO IT JUST SO SHE DOESN'T HAVE TO PLAY WITH **RANDOS.**

SORRY, BABE, THIS IS TAKING LONGER THAN I THOUGHT. CAN YOU EMPTY THE DISHWASHER WHILE I FINISH UP?

UGH, **FINE.**

MY MOM AND DAD SPLIT WHEN I WAS JUST TWO, SO IT'S JUST **ME AND HER** NOW.

MOM AND DAD GOT MARRIED WHEN THEY WERE REALLY YOUNG, BUT I DON'T THINK THEY WERE A GOOD MATCH. HE'S...A PRETTY *BORING* DUDE, LOL.

HONESTLY, I THINK MOM'S *PARENTS* LIKED MY DAD MORE THAN *SHE* DID!

DAD LIVES IN EDMONTON NOW FOR WORK, AND HE'S REAL BUSY, SO I ONLY SEE HIM ABOUT ONCE A *YEAR.*

I ONLY HAVE ONE SET OF GRANDPARENTS-- MY MOM'S FOLKS. THEY'RE REALLY OLD-FASHIONED AND *STRICT,* THOUGH.

THEY RETIRED TO THE ISLAND, SO I DON'T SEE THEM MUCH, EITHER, WHICH IS HONESTLY FINE BY ME. I MEAN, I LOVE THEM, BUT MAN ARE THEY *JUDGY!*

PRIYA ASKED ONCE IF I MISS HAVING A BIG FAMILY, BUT HOW CAN YOU MISS SOMETHING YOU'VE NEVER REALLY *HAD?* FOR AS LONG AS I CAN REMEMBER, IT'S JUST BEEN ME AND MY MOM AND THAT'S ALL I *NEED!*

OKAY, LET'S FINISH GETTING THIS KITCHEN TIDY, SO WE CAN *WRECK* IT UP AGAIN!

YES!!

HAHAHA!

LET'S GET READY TO BBB!!

BBB IS THIS FUN TRADITION WE DO ONCE EVERY OTHER FRIDAY. IT STANDS FOR BIBIMBAP, BINGSU, AND BINGEING!

IT'S BASICALLY JUST DINNER, DESSERT, AND TV, BUT MORE FUN?

BIBIMBAP IS A KOREAN DISH THAT IS AWESOME.

VEGGIES AND MEAT AND FRIED EGG ON RICE WITH A SWEET AND SPICY SAUCE. MOM MAKES IT SO GOOD.

THE BEST PART OF KOREAN FOOD, THO, IS DEFINITELY THE BANCHAN (OR SIDE DISHES)! EVERY MEAL IS ALWAYS SERVED WITH AT LEAST A COUPLE!

WHEN I WAS LITTLE, WE VISITED KOREA WITH MY GRANDPARENTS, AND WE WENT TO THIS RESTAURANT THAT SERVED LIKE DOZENS OF DIFFERENT BANCHAN!!

17

MY FAVORITE SIDE DISH BY FAR IS *GAMJA BOKKEUM* (FRIED POTATOES IN A SWEET AND SALTY SAUCE), AND EVERY BBB NIGHT WHILE MOM DOES EVERYTHING ELSE, I GET TO MAKE IT! *HERE'S HOW!!*

INGREDIENTS--

2-3 MEDIUM POTATOES

2 GARLIC CLOVES

1 SMALL ONION

2 TBSP SOY SAUCE

1/2 CUP WATER

1 TBSP SESAME OIL

1 TBSP COOKING OIL

2 TBSP SUGAR

STEP ONE--PEEL POTATOES! CHOP 'EM INTO BITE-SIZE CHUNKS! (ABOUT AN INCH BIG.) DON'T MAKE THEM TOO SMALL!

STEP TWO--NOW CUT UP THE ONION INTO SAME-SIZE CHUNKS! TRY NOT TO *CRY!* (THIS IS IMPOSSIBLE.)

STEP THREE--RINSE THE HECK OUT OF THE POTATOES! WE WANT TO GET RID OF ALL THE STARCH WE CAN!

STEP FOUR--NOW CHUCK THE COOKING OIL AND POTATOES INTO A HOT FRYING PAN! THROW THE MINCED GARLIC IN THERE, TOO! *SIZZLE TIME!!*

(I USED TO BE SCARED OF HOT PANS, BUT ONCE YOU'VE USED ONE A COUPLE TIMES, YOU GET USED TO IT. *KINDA...*)

STEP FIVE--NOW CHUCK THE ONION IN THERE, TOO, AND STIR FOR A COUPLE OF MINUTES UNTIL THE SPUDS START LOOKING A BIT SEE-THROUGH!

STEP SIX--MAKE IT *SAUCY!!* ADD THE WATER, SOY SAUCE, AND SUGAR AND SIMMER FOR ABOUT TEN MINUTES.

KEEP STIRRING DURING THIS STEP! SUGAR BURNS, SO YOU GOTTA KEEP IT *MOVING!* (I LEARNED THE HARD WAY.)

STEP SEVEN--ONCE THE POTATO IS COOKED AND THE LIQUID IS EVAPORATED, PUT IT ALL IN A BOWL AND MIX IN THE SESAME OIL.

(IF YOU HAVE THEM, SPRINKLE SESAME SEEDS ON TOP TO MAKE IT LOOK *FANCY!*)

AND THAT'S *IT!* MY FAVORITE SIDE DISH FOR MY FAVORITE DINNER!! *EAT UP!!*

MEOK JA!!*

CLNK!

*KOREAN FOR "LET'S EAT!"

NOM NOM NOM NOM NOM NOM NOM NOM NOM NOM

MUNCH!

SLORP!

GULP!!

TEN MINUTES OF FURIOUS EATING LATER...

AAAHHHH...

SOOO... FULLLL...

TIME FOR *BINGSU!!*

NOOO...

HA HAHA!

COME *ON,* MOM!

CAN'T WE JUST SKIP IT AND GET STRAIGHT TO *BINGEING* SOMETHING?

NO WAY!! PUT YOUR *COAT* ON!!

FLOP!!

UHRR....

...AND THEN HE JUST GULPED DOWN THE *WHOLE THING!!*

AUGH, *YUCK!!*

WHAT DID YOU *DO?!*

WHAT *COULD* WE DO?? HE'D ALREADY EATEN IT, SO WE JUST LET HIS OWNER KNOW.

HE THOUGHT IT WAS *FUNNY* BUT SAID HE'D KEEP AN EYE ON HIM JUST IN CASE.

WELL, I HAVE TO SAY, I'M SO *IMPRESSED* BY THE WAY YOU GIRLS HAVE MADE *PAWS* SUCH A *SUCCESS!*

GABBY'S DAD TELLS ME THAT ALL OF YOUR CLIENTS ARE *THRILLED!*

WHEN I WAS YOUR AGE, I DEFINITELY WOULDN'T HAVE BEEN ABLE TO HANDLE ALL THAT *RESPONSIBILITY.*

DIDN'T YOU TELL ME YOU USED TO BE A *BABYSITTER* AT MY AGE? YOU WERE WATCHING LITERAL BABIES!

LIKE...TINY *HUMANS!!*

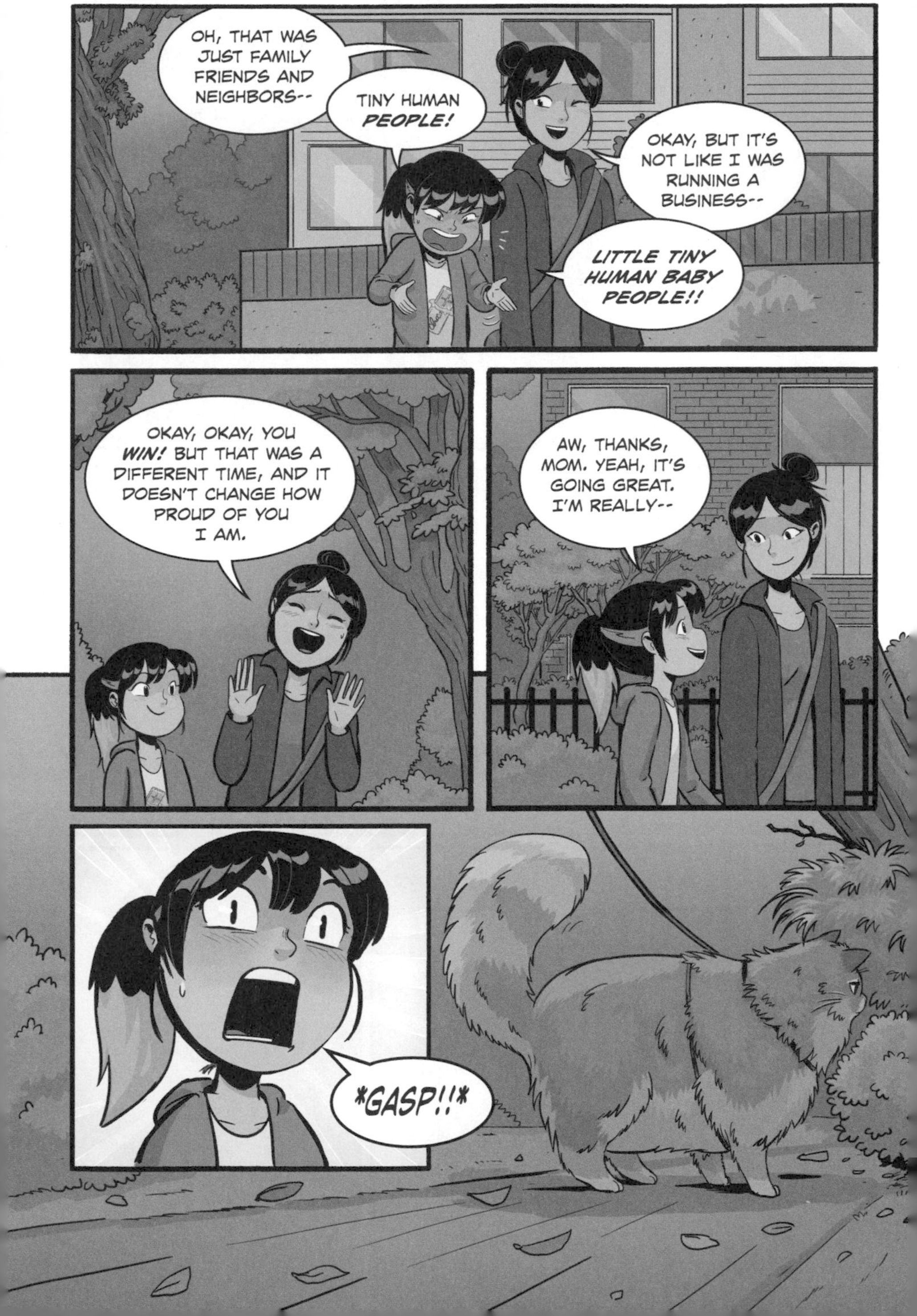
OH, THAT WAS JUST FAMILY FRIENDS AND NEIGHBORS--
TINY HUMAN PEOPLE!
OKAY, BUT IT'S NOT LIKE I WAS RUNNING A BUSINESS--
LITTLE TINY HUMAN BABY PEOPLE!!
OKAY, OKAY, YOU WIN! BUT THAT WAS A DIFFERENT TIME, AND IT DOESN'T CHANGE HOW PROUD OF YOU I AM.
AW, THANKS, MOM. YEAH, IT'S GOING GREAT. I'M REALLY--
GASP!!

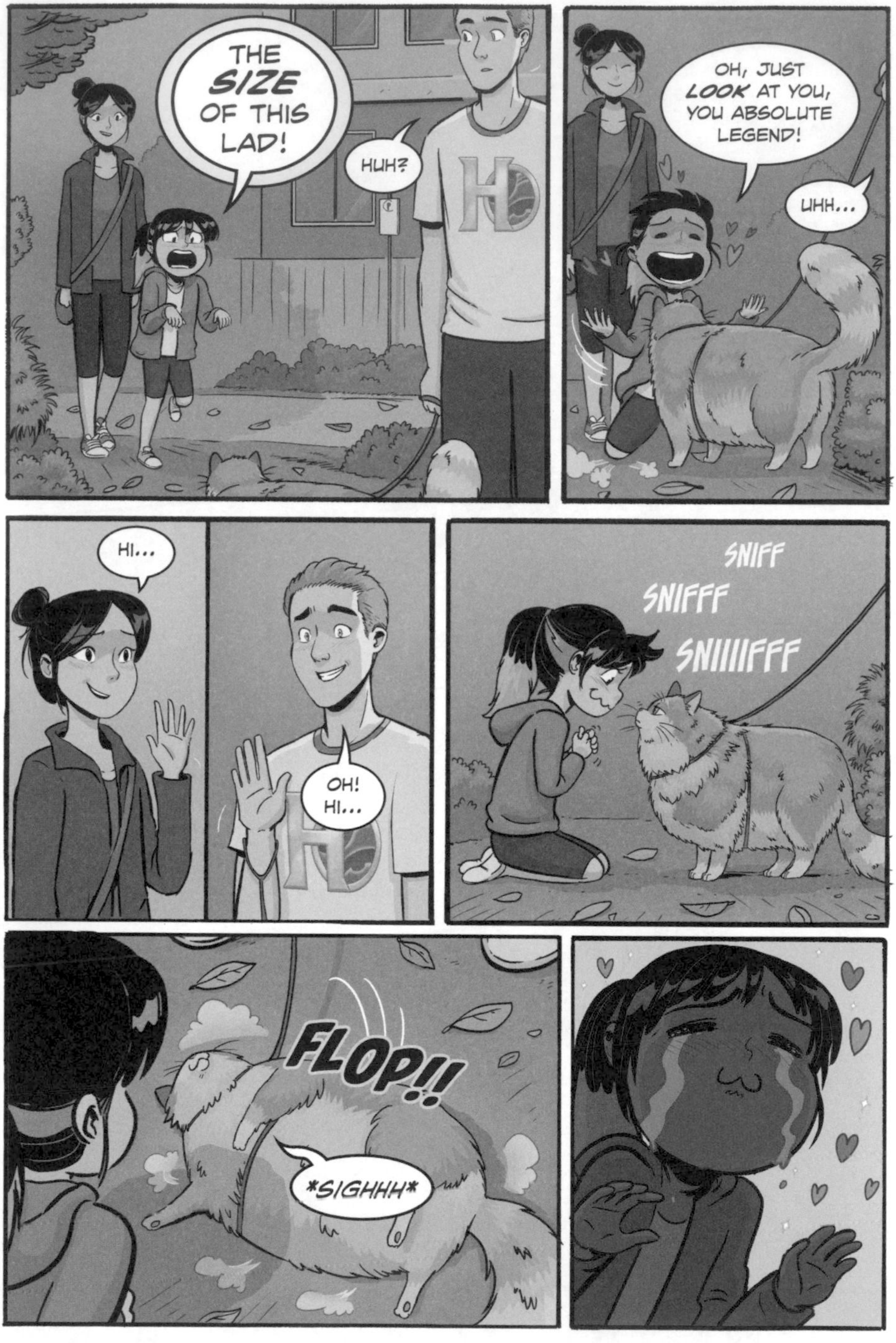
THE SIZE OF THIS LAD!
HUH?
OH, JUST LOOK AT YOU, YOU ABSOLUTE LEGEND!
UHH...
HI...
OH! HI...
SNIFF
SNIFFF
SNIIIIFFF
FLOP!!
SIGHHH

WHAT IS YOUR NAME, KING?

SORRY!! SHE HAS A...*THING* FOR ANIMALS!

HA! I CAN *TELL!*

THIS IS MY CAT, *CHONK.* WHAT'S *YOUR* NAME?

CHONK...

SKRTCH

YOUR NAME IS CHONK, *TOO?*

WHAT A COINCIDENCE!

GROAN

HAHA...MINDY! BE *NICE!*

SHE'S MINDY, AND I'M SUNNY!

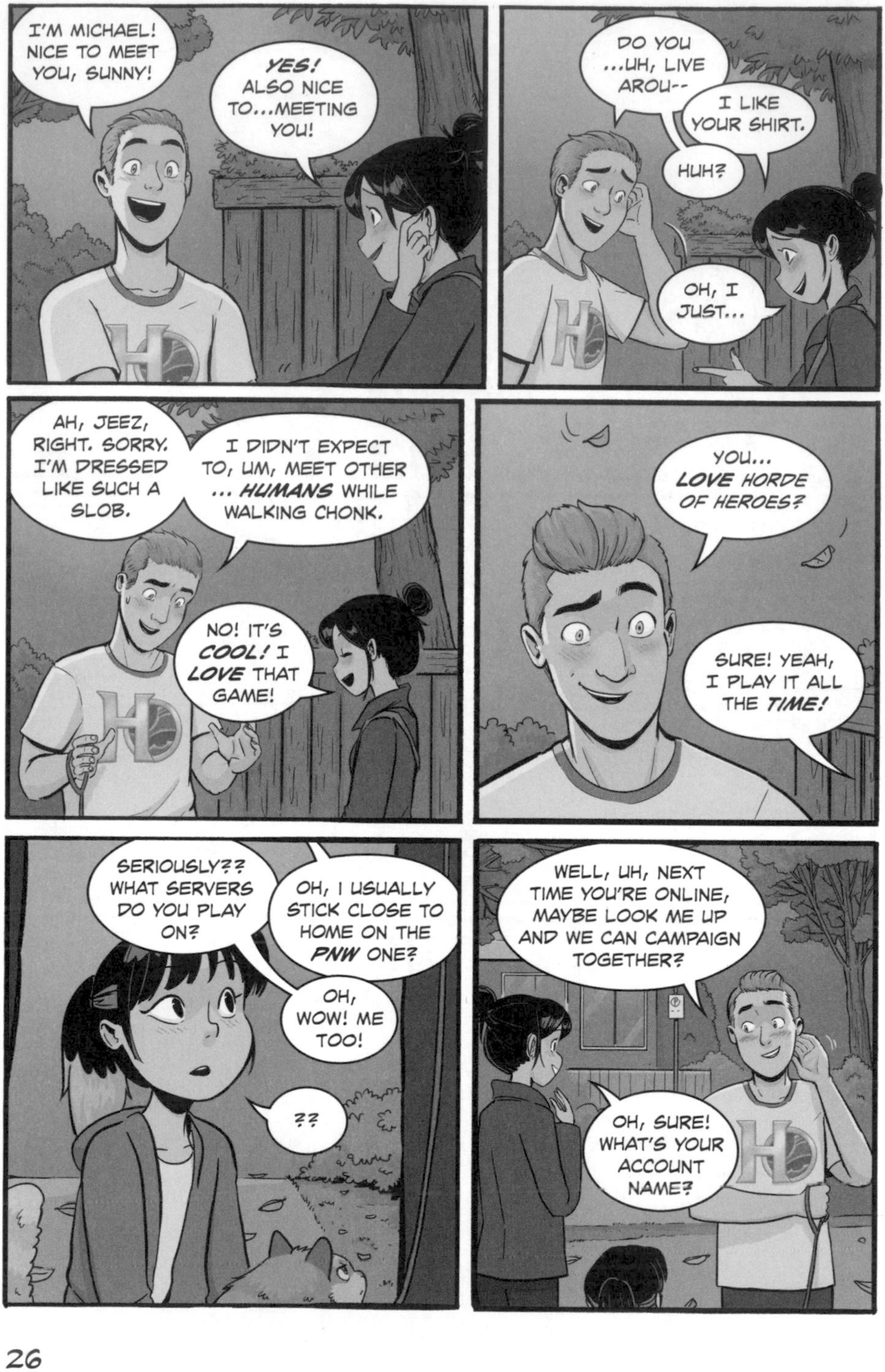
I'M MICHAEL! NICE TO MEET YOU, SUNNY!
YES! ALSO NICE TO...MEETING YOU!
DO YOU ...UH, LIVE AROU--
I LIKE YOUR SHIRT.
HUH?
OH, I JUST...
AH, JEEZ, RIGHT. SORRY. I'M DRESSED LIKE SUCH A SLOB.
I DIDN'T EXPECT TO, UM, MEET OTHER ... HUMANS WHILE WALKING CHONK.
NO! IT'S COOL! I LOVE THAT GAME!
YOU... LOVE HORDE OF HEROES?
SURE! YEAH, I PLAY IT ALL THE TIME!
SERIOUSLY?? WHAT SERVERS DO YOU PLAY ON?
OH, I USUALLY STICK CLOSE TO HOME ON THE PNW ONE?
OH, WOW! ME TOO!
??
WELL, UH, NEXT TIME YOU'RE ONLINE, MAYBE LOOK ME UP AND WE CAN CAMPAIGN TOGETHER?
OH, SURE! WHAT'S YOUR ACCOUNT NAME?

OH, GOD.

IT'S...UH...UM, "MIKELIKESHIKES"?

HAHA HA!

OHHHKAY, WELL, WE'D BETTER GET *GOING.*

OH, UH, YEAH, OKAY...BYE, MICHAEL! MAYBE I'LL SEE YOU *ONLINE!*

OKAY, *BYE!!* I HOPE SO!

BYE, *CHONK!!*

??

WHAT?

UGH.

WHAT?!

COME **ON,** MOM! YOU'VE BARELY TOUCHED YOUR **MANGO GO-GO!**

HUH? OH, SORRY. GUESS I'M JUST NOT THAT HUNGRY.

YOU'RE THINKING ABOUT THAT DORK WE MET, AREN'T YOU?

HE WASN'T A **DORK!!** I THOUGHT HE WAS **COOL!**

PFFFT! WHATEVER...

LOOK, DO YOU WANT MY **DESSERT** OR SHOULD WE JUST **GO?**

GIMME!

SLORP! SLUP!

ALL RIGHT! LET'S GET READY TO *BINGE*!!

FLOP!!

WHAT DO YOU FEEL LIKE WATCHING??

OH, UH...

ANYTHING'S OKAY WITH ME. WHY DON'T *YOU* PICK SOMETHING?

I...I JUST NEED TO GO CHECK SOMETHING...ON THE COMPUTER.

WHAT?! BUT IT'S *BBB* NIGHT!

I KNOW!! IT'LL JUST TAKE A *SECOND*!!

TIK TEKKA TEKKA TIK CLIK CLIK

29

MONDAY MORNING...

HEY, PRIYA!

HEY, GABS!

HOW WAS SOCCER...UH, REHEARSAL YESTERDAY?

"REHEARSAL"?

IS... THAT NOT RIGHT?

I THINK YOU KNOW IT IS NOT.

HAHA...FINE, "PRACTICE"? HOW WAS PRACTICE, THEN?

DID YOU KICK ANY GOOD... SCORES?

PLEASE JUST STOP.

FINE... YOU CAN'T SAY I DIDN'T TRY, THO!

HA HA HA!

OH!

--THINK YOU'RE GOING TO LIKE IT HERE AT BRONTË.

HI, *HAZEL!* PLEASURE TO MEET YOU.

I'M YOUR TEACHER, MS. MIRANDA.

WHY DON'T YOU SET UP AT THIS TABLE FOR NOW AND WE'LL GET YOU SETTLED IN A MINUTE?

I JUST NEED TO TALK TO PRINCIPAL SINGH FOR A SEC.

LET'S GO *OVER!*

UM, HI.

HI.

OH! *HI!*

I'M PRIYA.

I'M GABBY!

I'M *HAZEL!*

ARE YOU ... UH, GONNA BE JOINING THIS CLASS?

JEEZ, I HOPE SO, OR I'M IN THE WRONG *ROOM!*

HAHA-- YEAH, SILLY QUESTION.

MY FAMILY JUST MOVED HERE FROM *CALGARY.* MY MOM GOT A NEW JOB HERE.

OH, OKAY. IS... UH, CALGARY ...NICE?

I GUESS? THE *WINTERS* SURE SUCK.

HA, YEAH, I BET.

...

!!

OH, *HEY!* IS THAT *HORNS OF DESTINY*?? YOU'VE ALREADY GOT THE FIFTH BOOK?

YEAH! IT CAME OUT LAST WEEK! HAVE YOU READ ANY OF THE *OTHER* BOOKS?

OF COURSE! I'M A *HUGE* HORNHEAD.

TEAM *LIGHTFEATHER* ALL THE WAY!

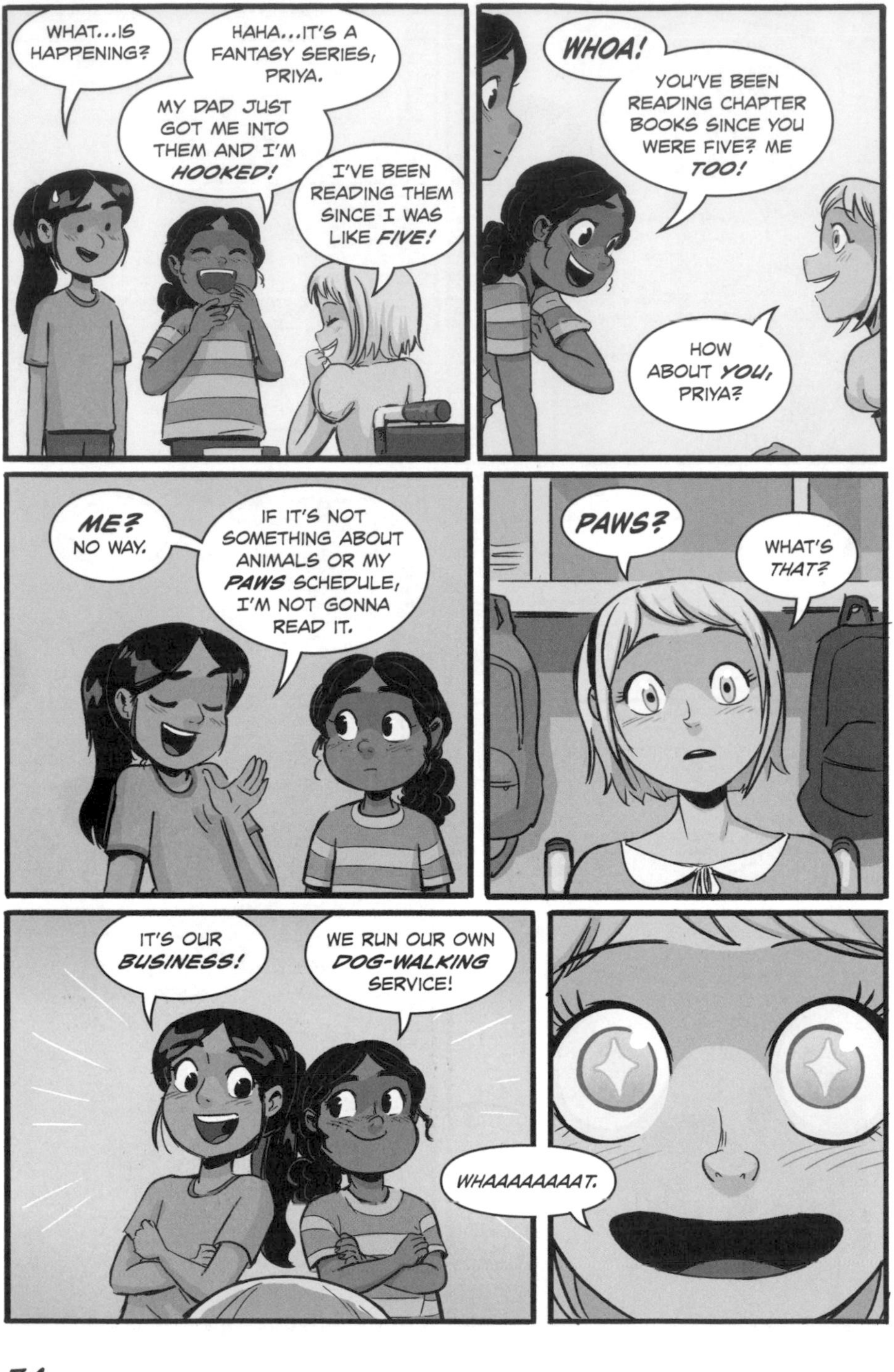
WHAT...IS HAPPENING?
HAHA...IT'S A FANTASY SERIES, PRIYA.
MY DAD JUST GOT ME INTO THEM AND I'M *HOOKED!*
I'VE BEEN READING THEM SINCE I WAS LIKE *FIVE!*
WHOA!
YOU'VE BEEN READING CHAPTER BOOKS SINCE YOU WERE FIVE? ME *TOO!*
HOW ABOUT *YOU,* PRIYA?
ME? NO WAY.
IF IT'S NOT SOMETHING ABOUT ANIMALS OR MY *PAWS* SCHEDULE, I'M NOT GONNA READ IT.
PAWS?
WHAT'S *THAT?*
IT'S OUR *BUSINESS!*
WE RUN OUR OWN *DOG-WALKING* SERVICE!
WHAAAAAAAAT.

THAT'S *AMAZING!*

I *LOVE* DOGS!

I'M *OBSESSED* WITH THEM!

HOW MANY DOGS DO YOU *HAVE??*

HOW MANY MEMBERS IN YOUR *CLUB??*

DO--

BANG!!

?!

GRRR...

BAUGH!!

WHOA... THAT'S A *LOT* OF DRAMA.

HAHA, YEAH, THAT'S MINDY. SHE'S IN *PAWS,* TOO. SHE'S NOT USUALLY THIS *EXTRA,* THO!

YEAH, I THINK WE'D BETTER GO SEE WHAT'S *UP...*

OKAY! BYE! NICE MEETING YOU!

CAN'T WAIT TO HEAR MORE ABOUT *PAWS!*

SHE SEEMS *COOL!*

I *KNOW,* RIGHT?

HEY THERE, MINDY. EVERYTHING ...UH, OKAY?

NO.

WHAT'S THE *MATTER?*

YEAH, WE BARELY *HEARD* FROM YOU ALL WEEKEND.

UGH! OKAY, *SO!* YOU KNOW HOW FRIDAY NIGHT WAS SUPPOSED TO BE *GIRLS'* NIGHT--JUST ME AND MY *MOM?*

YEAH...

WELL, WHEN WE WERE OUT THAT NIGHT, WE RAN INTO SOME *GUY.*

EW. WAS HE LIKE A *CREEP* OR SOMETHING?

WHAT? NO, NOTHING LIKE THAT. HE'S JUST SOME *DORK.*

OKAY...SO... WHAT'S THE *PROBLEM?*

36

THE PROBLEM IS THAT SHE SPENT ALL THE REST OF THAT NIGHT *THINKING* ABOUT HIM!

AND THAT'S BAD BECAUSE...

BECAUSE IT WAS SUPPOSED TO BE *OUR* NIGHT! SHE KEPT CHECKING HER COMPUTER--

THEY BOTH PLAY THIS WEIRD *GAME* AND WERE LIKE CHATTING WITH EACH OTHER ON THE APP--

THAT SOUNDS KIND OF NICE--

IT DOES *NOT!*

"IT WENT ON ALL *WEEKEND!* THE NEXT DAY, SHE WAS EITHER PLAYING *VIDEO GAMES* WITH HIM..."

...OR *TEXTING* WITH HIM ALL DAY."

37

"GUYS, SHE ACTUALLY *CALLED* HIM.

ON THE *PHONE.*"

EW, WHUT.

OLD PEOPLE ARE SO *WEIRD.*

I *KNOW,* RIGHT?!

...AND THAT'S NOT THE *WORST* PART.

WHAT'S THE *WORST* PART?

SHE WENT ON A *DATE...*

AND I HAD TO *COME!!*

"OH, SURE--MOM SAID IT *WASN'T* A DATE AND THAT WE WERE JUST MEETING HER NEW FRIEND FOR LUNCH...

...BUT I KNOW A DATE WHEN I SEE ONE!!"

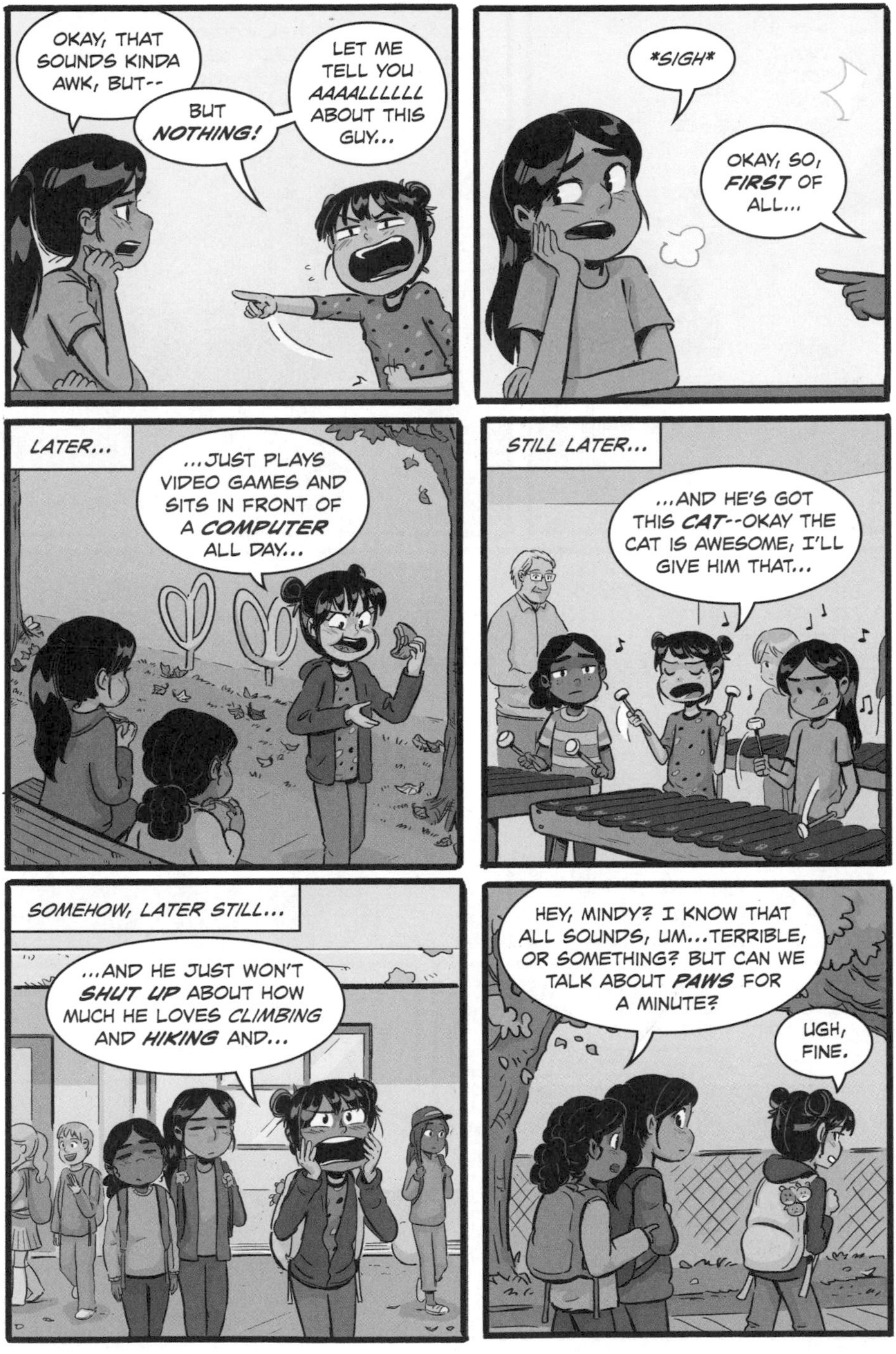

OKAY, THAT SOUNDS KINDA AWK, BUT--
BUT NOTHING!
LET ME TELL YOU AAAALLLLLL ABOUT THIS GUY...
SIGH
OKAY, SO, FIRST OF ALL...
LATER...
...JUST PLAYS VIDEO GAMES AND SITS IN FRONT OF A COMPUTER ALL DAY...
STILL LATER...
...AND HE'S GOT THIS CAT--OKAY THE CAT IS AWESOME, I'LL GIVE HIM THAT...
SOMEHOW, LATER STILL...
...AND HE JUST WON'T SHUT UP ABOUT HOW MUCH HE LOVES CLIMBING AND HIKING AND...
HEY, MINDY? I KNOW THAT ALL SOUNDS, UM...TERRIBLE, OR SOMETHING? BUT CAN WE TALK ABOUT PAWS FOR A MINUTE?
UGH, FINE.

OKAY! *SO!* TO REVIEW--

WE NEED TO PICK UP A FEW NEW *CLIENTS!*

"GALE FINISHED HER WORK CRUNCH AND ONLY NEEDS US TO WALK *CORPORAL WAGS* ONCE OR TWICE A WEEK NOW..."

"...AND KAYLA IS GETTING A LOT BETTER AND CAN WALK *ROXY* ON HER OWN A FEW TIMES."

"GABBY, WE *KNOW* ALL OF THIS--"

"HUSH, DON'T INTERRUPT MY *PROCESS.*"

IT'S *RUDE* TO RUSH A GIRL WHEN SHE'S TELLING A STORY, YOU KNOW...

OH, BROTHER...

"*ANYWAY,* DAD AND I PUT UP ANOTHER BATCH OF FLIERS ON SATURDAY AND WE'VE ALREADY HAD TWO *OUTSTANDING* APPLICANTS!"

NOW!!

"*MEI* IS A SWEET OLD LADY WHO LIVES JUST DOWN THE STREET FROM *YOU*, MINDY.

SHE HAS A BIT OF TROUBLE GETTING AROUND AND WANTS SOME HELP WALKING HER GOOD GIRL, *DODY.*

PAWS (Pretty Awesome Walkers) 604-555-2445

DAD AND I WENT OVER TO HER PLACE LAST NIGHT AND SORTED IT *ALL* OUT.

(WELL, *DAD* SORTED IT OUT--I MOSTLY JUST ATE OLD-LADY HARD CANDIES.)

DODY IS THIS BIG OLD POODLE AND...WELL, YOU KNOW HOW SOME PEOPLE *LOOK* LIKE THEIR PETS?

YEAH, THAT'S *MEI* AND *DODY!*"

41

"THE OTHER CALL WE GOT WAS FROM A GUY NAMED *MARWOOD.*

I GUESS HE'S SOME KIND OF *BLUES* MUSICIAN?

MAYBE BLUES MUSIC DOESN'T *PAY* SO HOT, THOUGH, SINCE HE TEACHES MUSIC FROM NOON TO NIGHT EVERY DAY.

HE'D LOVE IT IF WE COULD TAKE HIS SHORT KING NAMED *CHAMPION JACK* FOR WALKS AFTER SCHOOL AND THEN FEED HIM WHEN WE DROP HIM OFF."

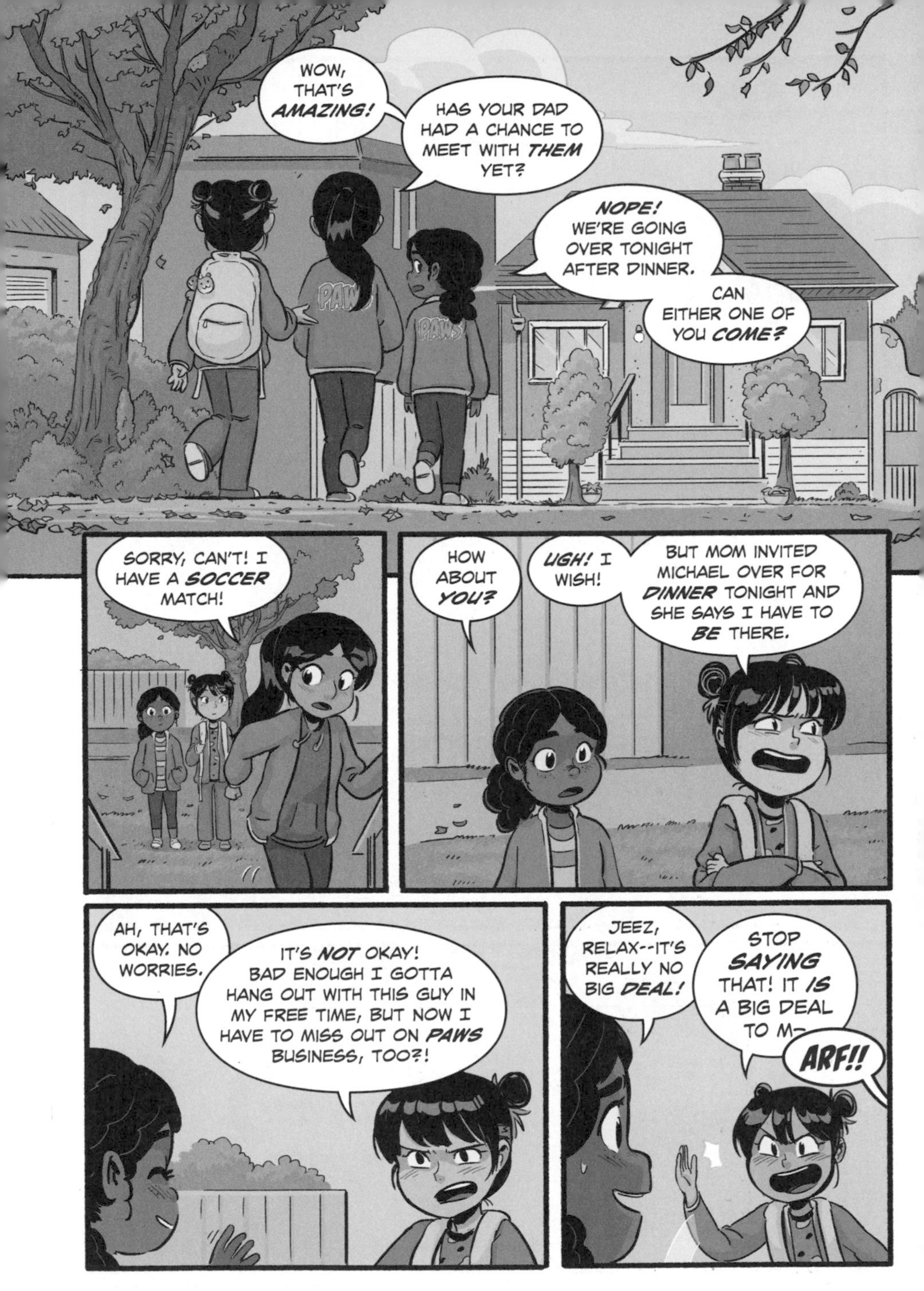
WOW, THAT'S AMAZING!
HAS YOUR DAD HAD A CHANCE TO MEET WITH THEM YET?
NOPE! WE'RE GOING OVER TONIGHT AFTER DINNER.
CAN EITHER ONE OF YOU COME?
SORRY, CAN'T! I HAVE A SOCCER MATCH!
HOW ABOUT YOU?
UGH! I WISH!
BUT MOM INVITED MICHAEL OVER FOR DINNER TONIGHT AND SHE SAYS I HAVE TO BE THERE.
AH, THAT'S OKAY. NO WORRIES.
IT'S NOT OKAY! BAD ENOUGH I GOTTA HANG OUT WITH THIS GUY IN MY FREE TIME, BUT NOW I HAVE TO MISS OUT ON PAWS BUSINESS, TOO?!
JEEZ, RELAX--IT'S REALLY NO BIG DEAL!
STOP SAYING THAT! IT IS A BIG DEAL TO M—
ARF!!

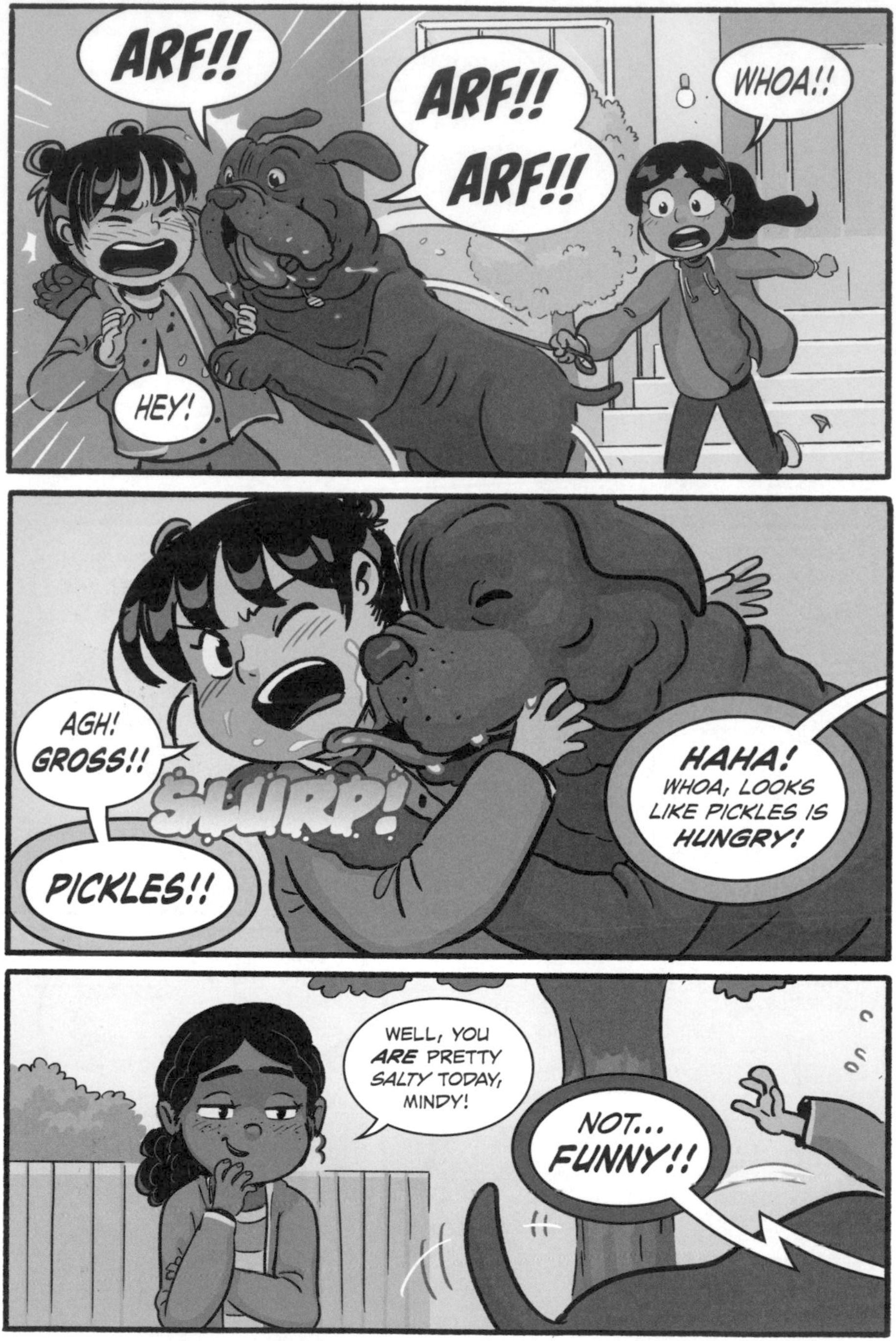

ARF!!
ARF!! ARF!!
WHOA!!
HEY!
AGH! GROSS!!
SLURP!
PICKLES!!
HAHA! WHOA, LOOKS LIKE PICKLES IS HUNGRY!
WELL, YOU ARE PRETTY SALTY TODAY, MINDY!
NOT... FUNNY!!

OKAY, CUT IT OUT, BIG GIRL! WHAT'S GOTTEN *INTO* YOU TODAY?

YUCK.

SORRY, MINDY. YOU OKAY?

I'M *FINE.*

OH, DON'T BE LIKE *THAT...*

I SAID I'M FINE!

I GOTTA PICK UP *SCRAPS.*

I'LL MEET YOU GUYS AT THE PARK.

THAT NIGHT...

HM-HMMM

KNOCK!
KNOCK!
KNOCK!

OH! MINDY, THAT'S MICHAEL! CAN YOU GET THE DOOR?

UGGH...

HEYA, KIDDO! HOW ARE--

MOM'S IN THE KITCHEN.

SNIFF
SNIFF

ITALIAN FOOD? AW, NUTS...

MICHAEL! HI!!

HI!

WHAT'S *THAT* YOU'VE GOT?

OH, IT'S... UH...

I DIDN'T KNOW WHAT WE'D BE HAVING...

SO, UM, IT'S KIMCHI? FROM MY FAVORITE KOREAN PLACE, *JANG MO JIB?*

OH, SO YOU JUST *ASSUMED* WE'D BE EATING KOREAN FOOD BECAUSE WE'RE KOREAN?

NO!

NO, I--I JUST...YOU TOLD ME ABOUT YOUR BIBIMBAP NIGHT AND--AND...

IT'S FINE!

MINDY, CAN YOU PLEASE FINISH SETTING THE TABLE?

BUT--

GO.

HOW ON EARTH DID YOU GET TAKEAWAY KIMCHI FROM *JANG MO JIB?*

I HAPPEN TO KNOW THEY WON'T *SELL* IT!

OH, WELL, IT WASN'T EASY. I HAD TO TELL THEM I WAS TRYING TO IMPRESS A *GIRL*...

SUS...

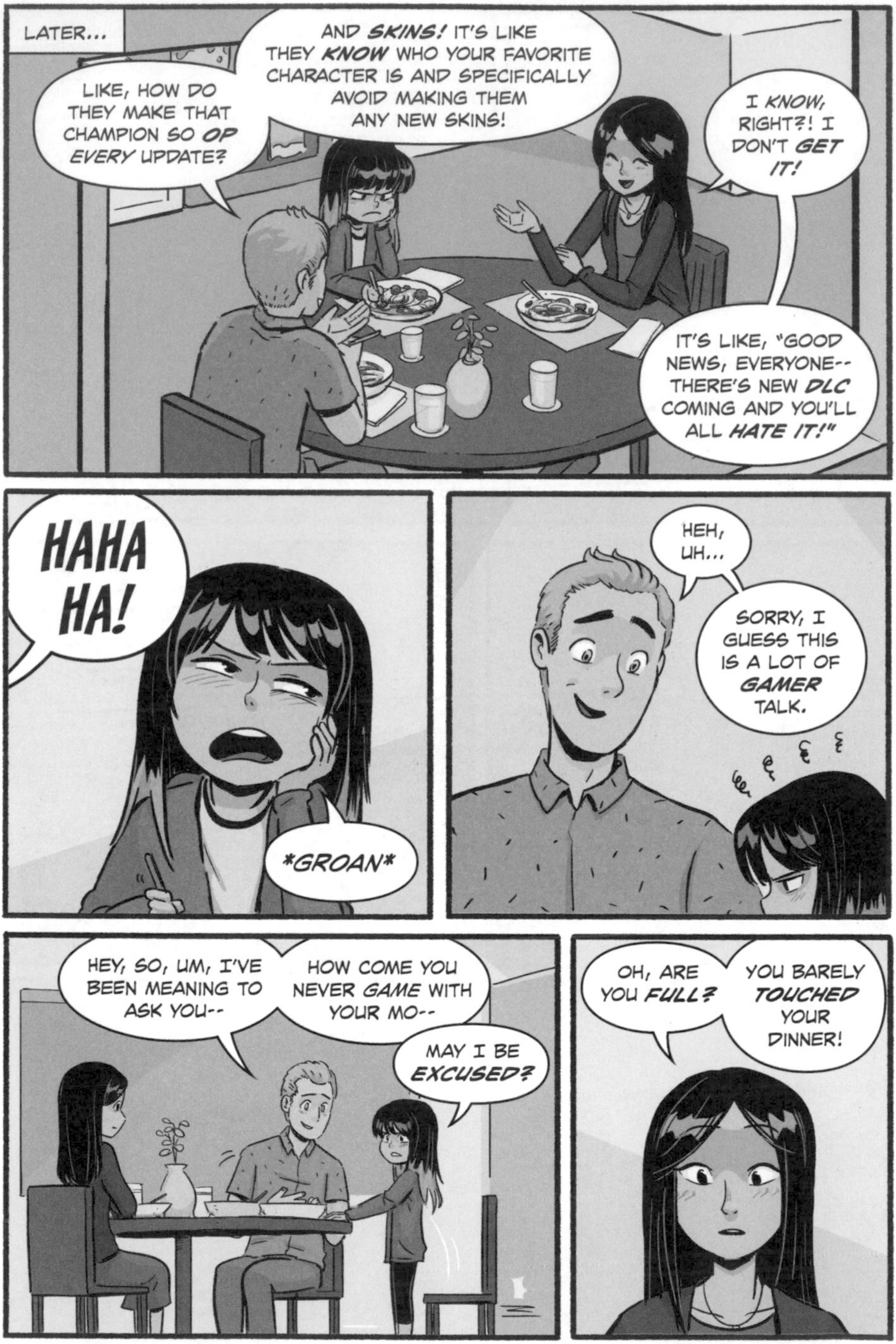
LATER...
LIKE, HOW DO THEY MAKE THAT CHAMPION SO *OP* *EVERY* UPDATE?
AND *SKINS!* IT'S LIKE THEY *KNOW* WHO YOUR FAVORITE CHARACTER IS AND SPECIFICALLY AVOID MAKING THEM ANY NEW SKINS!
I *KNOW,* RIGHT?! I DON'T *GET IT!*
IT'S LIKE, "GOOD NEWS, EVERYONE-- THERE'S NEW *DLC* COMING AND YOU'LL ALL *HATE IT!*"
HAHA HA!
GROAN
HEH, UH...
SORRY, I GUESS THIS IS A LOT OF *GAMER* TALK.
HEY, SO, UM, I'VE BEEN MEANING TO ASK YOU--
HOW COME YOU NEVER *GAME* WITH YOUR MO--
MAY I BE *EXCUSED?*
OH, ARE YOU *FULL?*
YOU BARELY *TOUCHED* YOUR DINNER!

YEAH, I'M REALLY NOT THAT HUNGRY.

ARE YOU SURE?

WE'VE GOT YOUR FAVORITE FROM EARNEST ICE CREAM FOR DESSERT.

NO, THANKS.

IS EVERY-THING OKAY, BABE?

YEAH, EVERYTHING IS *FINE.*

I JUST HAVE A LOT OF HOMEWORK TO DO.

SLAM!!

MAN, AFTER MICHAEL LEFT, MOM WAS SO ANNOYED WITH ME. BUT *WHATEVER!*

IT'S NOT *MY* FAULT HER NEW BOYFRIEND IS A TOTAL *LOSER.*

OMG, GIRLS, JUST WAIT UNTIL YOU HEAR ABOUT DINNER WITH MICHAEL LAST...

...NIGHT.

HI, MINDY!

UH, SO, MS. MIRANDA JUST SWITCHED UP THE TABLE GROUPS.

SHE SAID SHE WANTS YOU TO SWAP PLACES WITH HAZEL?

OH... I SEE.

SORRY! I--I DIDN'T *ASK* HER TO--

IT'S *FINE!*

YEAH, SHE MAKES *EVERYONE* CHANGE TABLES A COUPLE TIMES EVERY TERM!

OH. OKAY.

STILL, SORRY TO BREAK UP YOUR GROUP.

DON'T WORRY ABOUT IT, I GUESS...UM, HAZEL, RIGHT?

YEAH, UM...

SO, YOU'RE IN *PAWS*, TOO, RIGHT?

WHAT?

OH, UH, GABBY AND PRIYA TOLD ME ALL ABOUT *PAWS*. IT SOUNDS SO AMAZING!

YEAH, I MEAN...YEAH, IT'S AWESOME.

YOU'RE SO LUCKY! I'VE ALWAYS *WANTED* A DOG.

MY MOM SAYS SHE'S NOT SURE WE CAN REALLY HANDLE CARING FOR ONE.

THEY'RE A LOT OF WORK...

WHOA...PUMP THE BRAKES THERE, KID. IF YOU THINK WE'RE INVITING SOME RANDO TO JOIN *PAWS*, YOU CAN *FORGET* IT.

YEAH... THAT'S TOO BAD...

UM, WELL...

UH, SO WHAT WERE YOU SAYING WHEN YOU CAME IN, MINDY?

YEAH, WHAT'S UP? SOMETHING TO DO WITH THAT MICHAEL GUY?

MICHAEL?

WHO'S MICHAEL?

HE'S NOBODY. JUST SOME GUY.

ANYWAY, NEVER MIND.

MAYBE I'LL TELL YOU LATER WHEN WE'RE WALKING THE DOGS.

OH, WE ARE *DEFINITELY* GOING TO TALK ABOUT THIS LATER.

LATER...

...THE WHOLE MICHAEL THING WAS BAD ENOUGH, BUT NOW...

"BUT NOW" WHAT?

SIGH...WELL, I DUNNO, NOW WE'VE GOT THIS *NEW* GIRL...

YOU MEAN *HAZEL?*

WHAT'S WRONG WITH HAZEL?

OH, COME ON!

IT COULDN'T BE MORE *OBVIOUS* THAT SHE'S TRYING TO HORN IN ON *PAWS!*

WELL, MAYBE THAT'S NOT A *BAD* THING!

WITH MY SPORTS TAKING UP SO MUCH TIME, MAYBE WE COULD *USE* A NEW MEMBER.

NO *WAY!*

IT'LL UPSET OUR *WHOLE* SYSTEM!!

YOU CAN'T JUST GO INTRODUCING NEW PEOPLE INTO A GROUP LIKE--

HEY, *GUYS!*

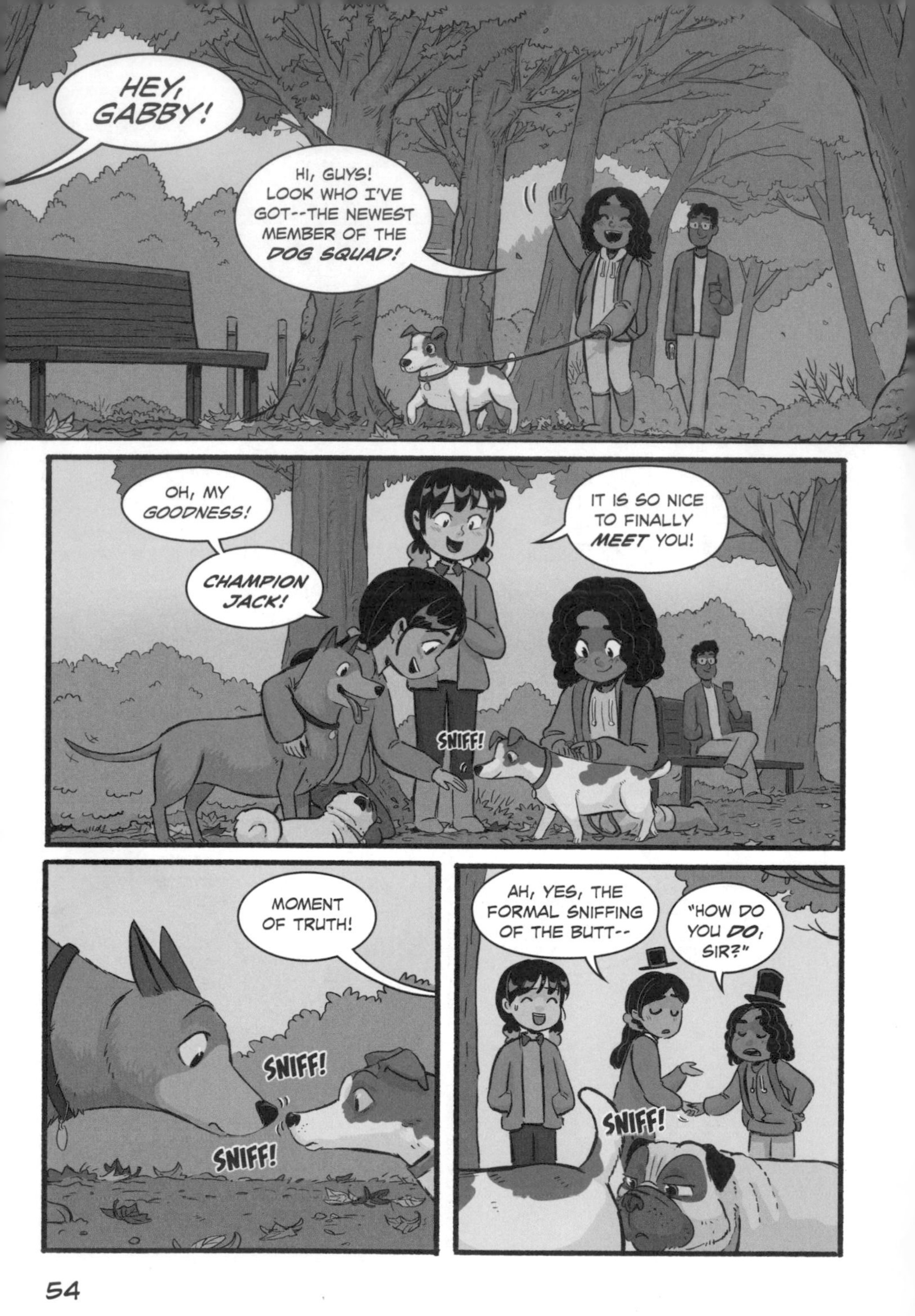
HEY, GABBY!
HI, GUYS! LOOK WHO I'VE GOT--THE NEWEST MEMBER OF THE DOG SQUAD!
OH, MY GOODNESS!
CHAMPION JACK!
IT IS SO NICE TO FINALLY MEET YOU!
SNIFF!
MOMENT OF TRUTH!
SNIFF!
SNIFF!
AH, YES, THE FORMAL SNIFFING OF THE BUTT--
"HOW DO YOU DO, SIR?"
SNIFF!

"VERY WELL, MY GOOD MAN!"

"A PLEASURE TO MAKE YOUR *ACQUAINTANCE!*"

"GENTLEMEN--PERHAPS YOU'D CARE TO JOIN ME IN A BIT OF *SPORT?*"

"CAPITAL IDEA, OLD BEAN!"

"DON'T MIND IF WE *DO!*"

HAHA!

YOU WERE SAYING SOMETHING ABOUT INTRODUCING *NEW MEMBERS* TO A GROUP?

OH, THAT'S TOTALLY *DIFFERENT!*

THEY'RE DOGS!

WHAT ARE YOU GUYS *TALKING* ABOUT?

MINDY THINKS HAZEL WANTS TO JOIN *PAWS*.

OH, HEY, THAT'S A GOOD *IDEA*, MINDY!

IT'S NOT MY IDEA!!

OKAY, FINE, BUT IT MIGHT STILL BE FUN. SHE'S *REALLY* FUNNY.

DO YOU THINK THE, UM, WHEELCHAIR MIGHT MAKE IT *HARD* FOR HER?

BEATS ME. I GUESS THAT'S FOR *HER* TO DECIDE, RIGHT?

SHE SEEMS TO GET AROUND PRETTY WELL IN IT.

YEAH, WE COULD JUST *ASK* HER--

NO ONE IS ASKING ANYONE! *PAWS* DOESN'T NEED ANOTHER MEMBER!

OKAY, BUT--

CAN WE JUST STOP *TALKING* ABOUT THIS?? IT'S HALLOWEEN SOON! I WANT TO TALK ABOUT *THAT!*

56

OKAAAY...WELL, MY DAD SAYS YOU SHOULD ALL COME TO MY PLACE FIRST FOR PIZZA AND DRINKS. HE SAID HE'D INVITE YOUR FOLKS, TOO.

THEN THE THREE OF US CAN ALL HEAD OUT TO TRICK-OR-TREAT TOGETHER?

UGH, SO YOU GUYS ARE STILL PLANNING ON DRESSING UP AND DOING ALL THAT?

YEAH! OF COURSE! FREE *CANDY*, MINDY!

PLUS, IT'S *FUN* TO DRESS UP!

WELL, I'LL COME ALONG, BUT I'M NOT DRESSING UP.

I THINK I'M A LITTLE TOO *OLD* FOR THAT, YOU KNOW?

MINDY, YOU'RE ELEVEN.

AND A *HALF!*

PFFT... MAN, YOU'RE *NUTS.*

I'M GONNA KEEP DRESSING UP TILL I'M LIKE *NINETY.*

I'LL LOOK SO OLD, I WON'T EVEN NEED A *COSTUME!*

HAHAHA!

HALLOWEEN!

...SO YOUR MOM AND BROTHERS WILL STOP BY LATER, PRIYA?

YEP, THE BOYS WANTED TO GET OUT TRICK-OR-TREATING RIGHT AWAY.

THEY DIDN'T EVEN EAT *DINNER!*

HA! SOUNDS LIKE *ME* WHEN I WAS A KID!

OH, YOU GIRLS LOOK SO *GOOD!!*

THANKS! WE'RE GOOD BOIS!

UH, I'M A GOOD *GIRL,* ACTUALLY.

DING-DONG! ♪ ♫

OH! OUR FIRST *TRICK-OR-TREATER!*

COMING!!

OH.

MY.

TRICK OR TREAT!

59

WOW! YOU GUYS LOOK *SO COOL!*

MINDY, I THOUGHT YOU SAID YOU WEREN'T GONNA DRESS...

...UP?

WHERE'S. THE PIZZA.

HOLY SMOKES! SUNNY, YOU LOOK GREAT!

AND YOU MUST BE MICHAEL?

YEAH! NICE TO *MEET* YOU!

HA, YOU ALL REALLY GOT IN THE *SPIRIT* OF THINGS, HEY?

BOO!

AW, YEAH-- HALLOWEEN'S MY *FAVORITE* HOLIDAY.

WHEN SUNNY SAID SHE AND MINDY WEREN'T DRESSING UP, I WENT STRAIGHT OUT AND GOT US THESE OUTFITS!

I'VE DRESSED UP EVERY HALLOWEEN OF MY LIFE! I'LL PROBABLY STILL BE DOING IT WHEN I'M *NINETY!!*

OMG, MINDY! THAT'S WHAT *PRIYA* SAI--

COME ON, GIRLSH! GRAB YOUR BAGSH. MFF! WE GOTTA GET GOING.

OH, OKAY!

BYE, MOM AND DAD!

MAKE SURE YOU GRAB A FLASHLIGHT!

YEAH, YEAH...I GOT IT!

MIGHT AS WELL GET THE OL' TREAT SACK WARMED UP...

GABBY...

BYEEE!!

SLAM!

SO, HE JUST SHOWED UP WITH THREE COSTUMES AND *FACE PAINT?*

YES! CAN *YOU* *BELIEVE* IT?

AND THEN HE WOULDN'T TAKE "NO" FOR AN ANSWER.

MOM THOUGHT IT WAS "SO FUN."

I MEAN, YOU GOTTA ADMIT--YOU GUYS *DID* LOOK PRETTY COOL.

NO, WE *DIDN'T!*

JEEZ, MINDY. I DON'T KNOW WHY THIS GUY *BUGS* YOU SO MUCH.

DING-DONG!

WHY, HELLO THER--

TRICK OR TREAT!!

HAHA! OKAY, HERE YA GO!

THANKS!

THANKS!

I MEAN, SURE, MICHAEL MIGHT BE A BIT OF A *DORK*, BUT THAT'S OKAY.

MY *DAD* IS A DORK, AND--

MICHAEL ISN'T MY *DAD!!*

WHOA! I--I WASN'T TRYING TO SAY HE *WAS.* I JUST...

H-HE'S JUST THIS *DUMB GUY* AND... A-AND...

...HE THINKS HE CAN JUST COME IN AND... A-AND--

AARGH!

OKAY, MINDY. IT'S OKAY. WE'RE SORRY THAT THIS HAS GOT YOU SO *UPSET.*

SIGH...

AH, I'M SORRY, TOO, GUYS.

I KNOW I'VE BEEN GOING ON AND *ON* ABOUT THIS. IT'S JUST...

IT'S JUST...FOR AS LONG AS I CAN REMEMBER, IT'S JUST BEEN ME AND MOM.

AND WE WERE REALLY *HAPPY!* OR, AT LEAST, *I* THOUGHT WE WERE.

AND EVERYTHING WITH *PAWS* AND YOU GUYS WAS GOING SO GREAT!

BUT...

♫ DING- DONG! ♫

BUT NOW IT JUST FEELS LIKE EVERYTHING'S CHANGING, AND I'M WORRIED THAT--

OMG! HI, GUYS!!

I CAN'T BELIEVE YOU'RE *HERE!*

...HAZEL??

HAHA--YEAH, IT'S ME! SORRY, I GUESS THE COSTUME IS A *LOT.*

HOW ARE YOU GUYS DOING?? GETTING LOTS OF CANDY??

WE'RE *GREAT!*

YEAH, LOTS!

WELL, LET ME HOOK YOU UP WITH SOME *MORE!*

HAHA! *SWEET!*

HOWDY!!

WHO DO WE HAVE *HERE?*

HEY, DAD.

THIS IS *GABBY* AND *PRIYA*, FROM SCHOOL.

THEY'RE--

AND *MINDY.*

OH! *MINDY!* I DIDN'T EVEN *RECOGNIZE* YOU! Y-YOU'RE SO *SCARY!*

MNN...

WELL, IT'S NICE TO *MEET* YOU GIRLS!

I'VE HEARD A LOT ABOUT Y--

DAD! PLEASE, GO AWAY!

OKAY, OKAY... *SHEESH*

SORRY...

SO, WHY AREN'T YOU OUT TRICK-OR-TREATING? ARE YOU TOO *COOL*, OR SOMETHING?

OH, DEFINITELY *NOT*.

NO ONE HAS *EVER* ACCUSED ME OF BEING TOO COOL.

NO, I...I DIDN'T REALLY HAVE ANYONE TO GO WITH, SO I FIGURED I'D JUST GIVE OUT CANDY AT THE DOOR THIS YEAR.

AH, WELL, THAT'S COOL.

ANYWAY! WE SHOULD BE GOI--

HEY, WHY DON'T YOU COME ALONG WITH *US?*

YEAH!

R-REALLY?

OF *COURSE!* COME ON! IT'LL BE *FUN*--RIGHT, GUYS?

YEAH...

WE JUST GOT STARTED, SO YOU HARDLY MISSED *ANYTHING!*

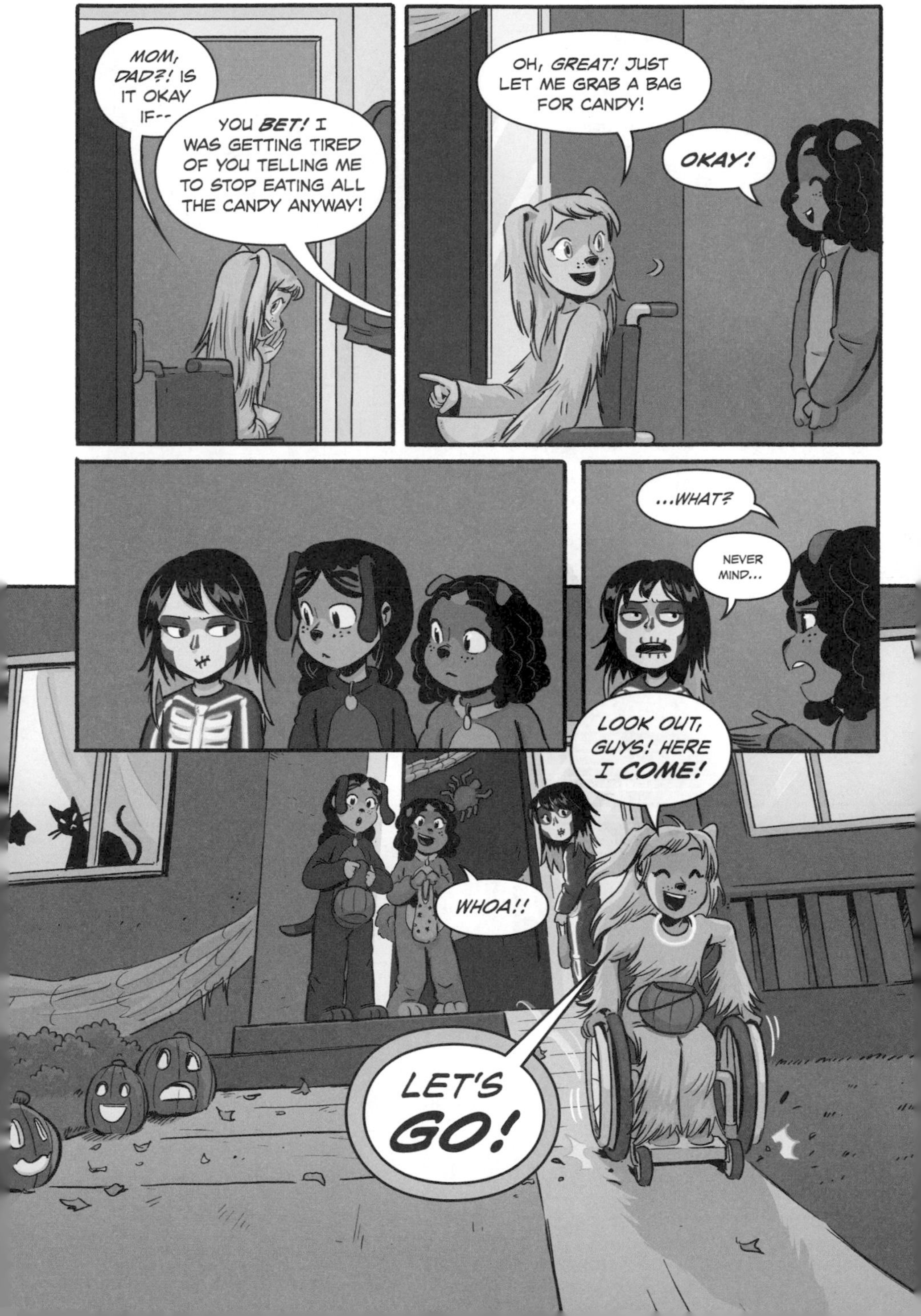
MOM, DAD?! IS IT OKAY IF--
YOU BET! I WAS GETTING TIRED OF YOU TELLING ME TO STOP EATING ALL THE CANDY ANYWAY!
OH, GREAT! JUST LET ME GRAB A BAG FOR CANDY!
OKAY!
...WHAT?
NEVER MIND...
LOOK OUT, GUYS! HERE I COME!
WHOA!!
LET'S GO!

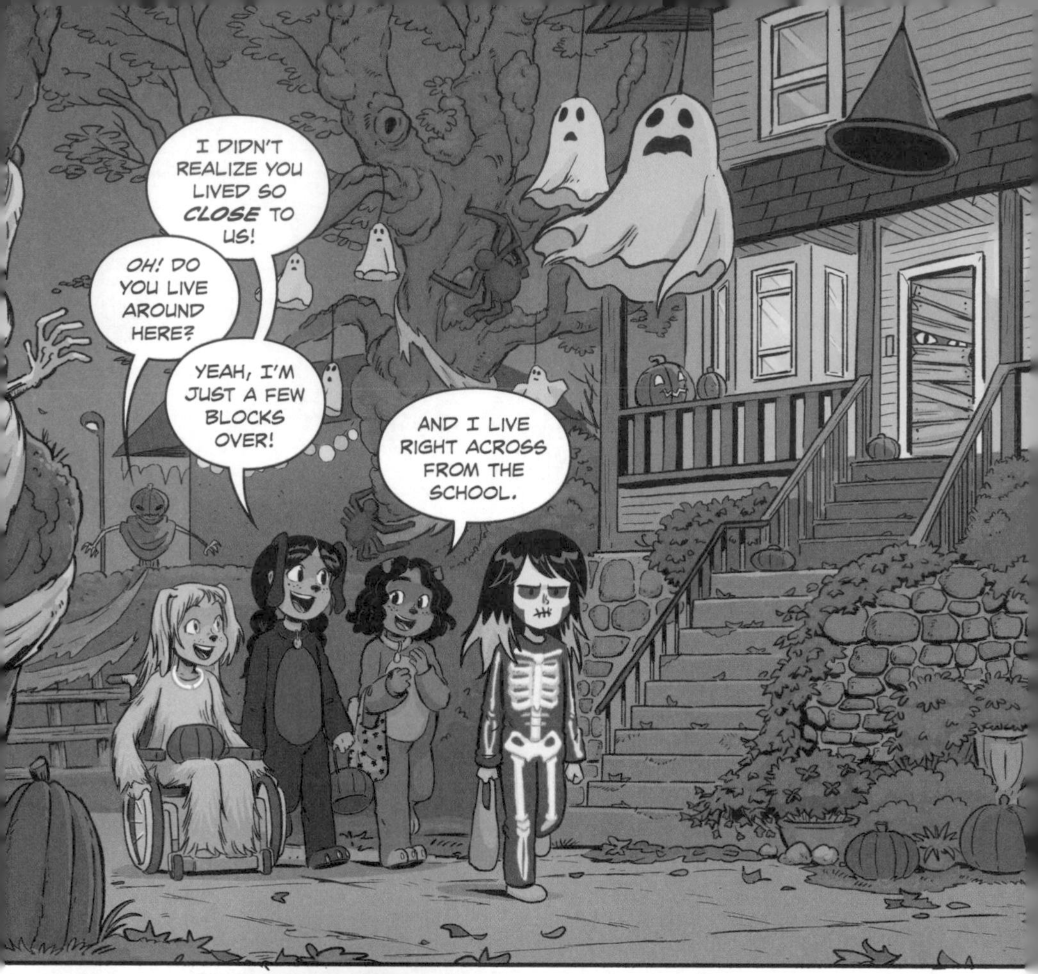
I DIDN'T REALIZE YOU LIVED SO *CLOSE* TO US!
OH! DO YOU LIVE AROUND HERE?
YEAH, I'M JUST A FEW BLOCKS OVER!
AND I LIVE RIGHT ACROSS FROM THE SCHOOL.

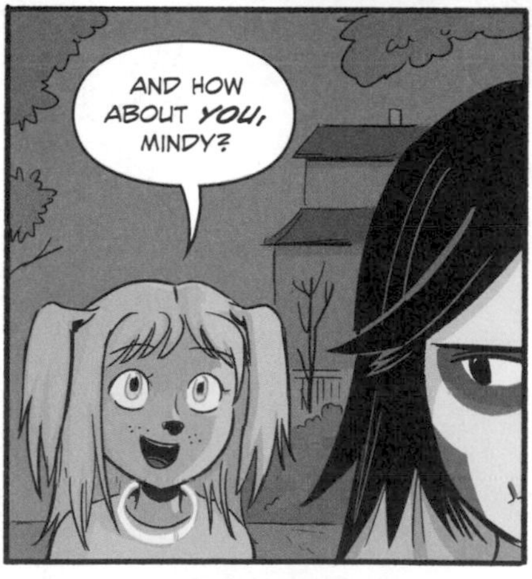
AND HOW ABOUT *YOU,* MINDY?

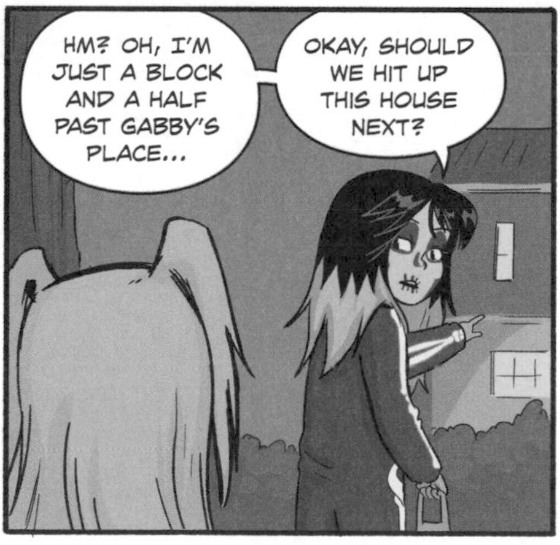
HM? OH, I'M JUST A BLOCK AND A HALF PAST GABBY'S PLACE...
OKAY, SHOULD WE HIT UP THIS HOUSE NEXT?

SURE!

OH, UH..., WHY DON'T YOU GUYS GO AHEAD? I'LL WAIT HERE!

HUH? WHAT ARE YOU *TALKING* ABOUT?

DON'T YOU WANT TO TRICK-OR-TREAT?

YEAH! IT'S JUST, WELL, I CAN'T GET UP THAT *PATH.*

AND THERE'S NO WAY I'M GETTING UP THE *STAIRS!*

OH, *JEEZ!* I DIDN'T EVEN *THINK--*

IT'S *FINE!* DON'T WORRY ABOUT IT!

LIKE *HECK.*

YEAH, IT IS DEFINITELY *NOT* FINE.

YOU WAIT RIGHT HERE A SEC.

71

DING-DONG!

TRICK OR TREAT!!

OH, HELLO!

TWO BUCKETS FOR YOU?

I GUESS YOU'VE GOT A REAL SWEET TOOTH, EH?

ACTUALLY, OUR FRIEND USES A WHEELCHAIR, AND YOUR HOUSE IS INACCESSIBLE TO HER.

HI, THERE!

TRICK OR TREAT!

OH!

OH MY!

I AM SO SORRY ABOUT THAT!

HERE'S YOUR BUCKET!

THANKS, GUYS!

NO *PROBLEM!* LET'S HOPE THE NEXT HOUSE IS A LITTLE EASIER FOR YOU!

YEAH...I KINDA DOUBT IT WILL BE.

HUH?

OH...

THIS *SUCKS!*

AH, I'M USED TO IT. MOST HOUSES AREN'T BUILT FOR WHEELCHAIRS.

I GUESS I NEVER REALLY LOOKED AT IT FROM YOUR PERSPECTIVE.

DON'T WORRY ABOUT IT! YOU GUYS KEEP TRICK-OR-TREATING!

I'M JUST HAPPY TO TAG ALONG!

FORGET *THAT!* WE'RE GONNA GET YOU CANDY FROM EVERY SINGLE *ONE* OF THESE HOUSES!

COME *ON!*

DING!

TRICK OR TREAT

HEL...

...LO?

TRICK OR TREAT!!

OH!

COMING!!

DONG!

TRICK OR TREAT!

?!

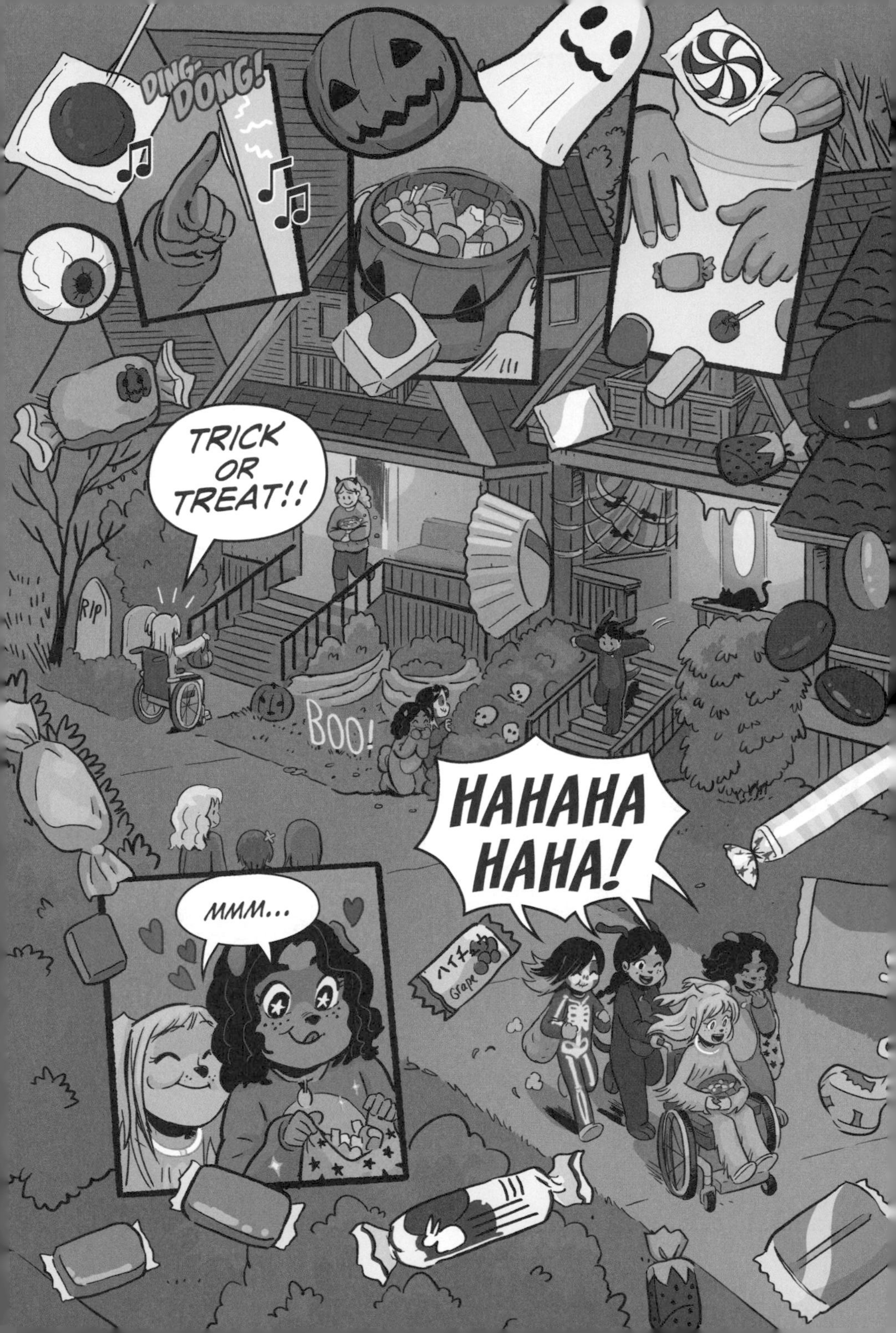
DING-DONG!
TRICK OR TREAT!!
BOO!
HAHAHA HAHA!
MMM...
Grape

HAHA...GUYS, I DON'T THINK WE CAN EVEN *CARRY* ANY MORE CANDY!

YEAH, I'M PRETTY MUCH *DONE* TRICKING AND TREATING.

OKAY-- JUST *ONE* LAST STOP!

YOU'RE GOING TO *LOVE* THIS, HAZEL!

JUST HANG ON!!

KNOCK!

KNOCK!

TRICK OR TREAT!!

GIRLS!!

HI, TERI! AWESOME COSTUME!

CAN WE SEE *PICKLES?*

PICKLES?

FOR... HALLOWEEN?

HAHA!

ARF!!

GO GET 'EM, GIRL!!

ARF!!

ARF!!

OKAY, I'M SORRY, BUT THIS... THIS IS DRIVING ME *NUTS*.

IT'S NOT THAT I DON'T *LIKE* HAZEL. IT'S REALLY *NOT!* SHE'S A NICE KID!

I JUST DON'T SEE WHY SHE HAS TO BE *OUR* FRIEND.

LIKE, WHAT IS IT ABOUT HER THAT GABBY AND PRIYA *LIKE* SO MUCH?

WHAT DOES *SHE* HAVE THAT *I DON'T?*

77

IT'S A FEELING THAT JUST WON'T GO *AWAY*. HAZEL'S SO *NICE* ALL THE TIME, BUT...I JUST CAN'T SHAKE THE IDEA THAT SHE'S TRYING TO TAKE MY SPOT ON *PAWS*.

MAYBE I'M JUST BEING *PARANOID*.

THEN AGAIN, MAYBE NOT.

HAHAHA!

HEY, GUYS.

OH, *THERE* YOU ARE! WHAT *TOOK* YOU?

HAD TO RETURN SOME MANGA TO THE LIBRARY.

WHAT ARE YOU LAUGHING ABOUT?

GABBY WAS JUST TELLING ME THE STORY OF THE TIME SHE TRIED TO WALK FIVE DOGS ALL BY *HERSELF!*

OH, HA. YEAH, THAT WAS SUCH A *MESS.*

I *BET!* BUT IT SOUNDS LIKE THINGS ARE GOING GREAT NOW, RIGHT?

UH, YEAH. THINGS ARE... GREAT.

IT WAS SO **COOL** TO GET TO MEET PICKLES!

SHE'S SO **CUTE!!**

YEAH, SHE'S GREAT!

I MEAN--SHE'S A HUGE, DROOLING MONSTER, BUT SURE...

YOU GUYS ARE SO **LUCKY** TO GET TO WALK THEM ALL EVERY **DAY!**

WELL, NOT **ALL** OF THEM--WE TRIED THAT AND IT DID NOT WORK OUT SO WELL.

YEAH, WE EACH WALK JUST ONE DOG A DAY.

BUT...DIDN'T YOU SAY THAT YOU HAVE **SEVEN** DOGS?

UH-OH, I SEE WHERE **THIS** IS GOING...

YEAH, BUT MOST DON'T NEED TO BE WALKED EVERY **DAY.**

REALLY? HAVE...UM, YOU EVER THOUGHT ABOUT ADDING ANOTHER **WALKER** TO YOUR CLUB?

JUST SO YOU CAN WALK THE DOGS MORE OFTEN, I MEAN?

ACTUALLY, WE **WERE** KINDA TH--

NO, I THINK WE'RE **FINE** JUST THE WAY WE ARE, ACTUALLY.

OH, YEAH! OF **COURSE!** JUST ASKING...

?

HEY, UM, ARE YOU GUYS BUSY ON SATURDAY?

WHYYY?

UH, WELL, IT'S JUST--MY BIRTHDAY WAS ACTUALLY LAST WEEK, JUST BEFORE HALLOWEEN.

AND, UM, MY MOM SAID WE COULD HAVE A BELATED BIRTHDAY PARTY AT MY HOUSE ON SATURDAY.

I MEAN-- IF YOU WANT? IT'S NO BIG DE--

I'D **LOVE** TO!

YEAH, ME TOO!

WAIT, WHAT **TIME?** I'VE GOT A SOCCER GAME AT NOON.

REALLY?! OH, MOM SAID YOU COULD COME AT AROUND *TWO* OR SO AND STAY FOR DINNER AND A MOVIE OR SOMETHING?

MY DAD PROMISED TO WORK IN THE GARAGE THE WHOLE TIME, HAHA!

HAHAHA!

YEAH, THAT WORKS!

MINDY, HOW ABOUT *YOU*?

THAT SOUNDS FUN, ACTUALLY.

IT SUCKS, BUT I'M *BUSY*...

OH, THAT'S OKAY...

BELIEVE ME, I'D RATHER COME TO YOUR PARTY. BUT MOM INSISTED I HAD TO DO THIS THING WITH HER AND MICHAEL...

REALLY? WHAT *IS* IT?

UGH!

IT'S *SO BORING!*

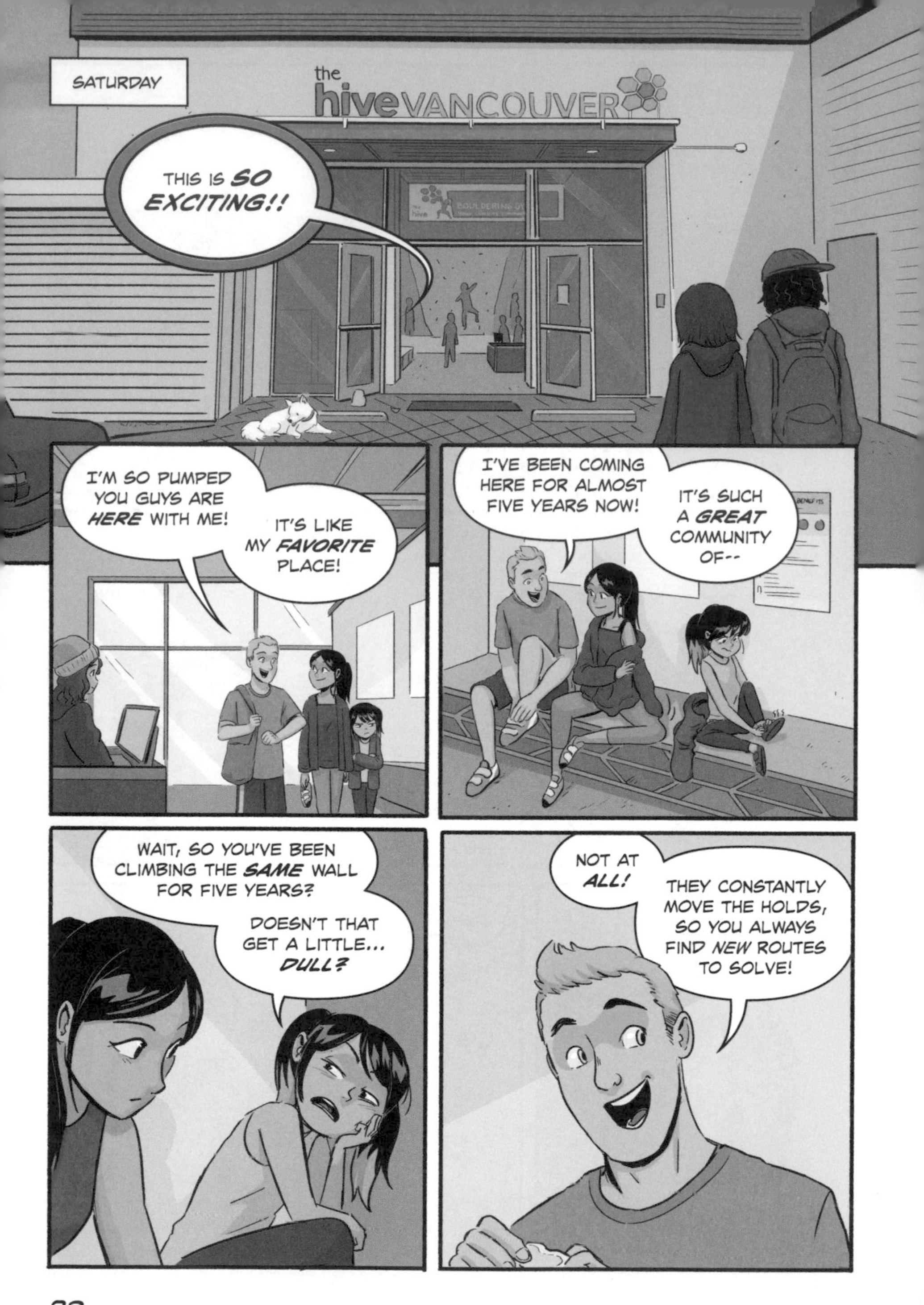
SATURDAY
the hive VANCOUVER
THIS IS SO EXCITING!!
I'M SO PUMPED YOU GUYS ARE HERE WITH ME!
IT'S LIKE MY FAVORITE PLACE!
I'VE BEEN COMING HERE FOR ALMOST FIVE YEARS NOW!
IT'S SUCH A GREAT COMMUNITY OF--
WAIT, SO YOU'VE BEEN CLIMBING THE SAME WALL FOR FIVE YEARS?
DOESN'T THAT GET A LITTLE... DULL?
NOT AT ALL!
THEY CONSTANTLY MOVE THE HOLDS, SO YOU ALWAYS FIND NEW ROUTES TO SOLVE!

"SOLVE"?

OH, YEAH! THAT'S WHAT WE--

I MEAN BOULDERERS--

PAT

PAT

--THAT'S WHAT WE *CALL* IT! A CHALLENGING ROUTE IS A "PROBLEM" THAT WE HAVE TO "SOLVE"!

YUCK

READY?

YUP!

OKAY, I KNOW A GREAT SECTION TO *START* ON.

REMEMBER WHAT I TOLD YOU?

USE YOUR *LEGS* TO PUSH UP. AND MAKE SURE TO PUT WEIGHT ON YOUR *TOES*, NOT THE MIDDLE OF YOUR FOOT.

YOUR SHOES ARE *BUILT* TO SUPPORT THE WEIGHT!

AND KEEP YOUR *HIPS* CLOSE TO THE WALL!

AND CLIMB WITH *STRAIGHT* ARMS. HANG FROM YOUR *FINGERS*. IF YOU BEND YOUR ARMS, YOU'LL *TIRE* FASTER. AND--

OKAY, OKAY! YEESH! ENOUGH ALREADY!

I'VE...

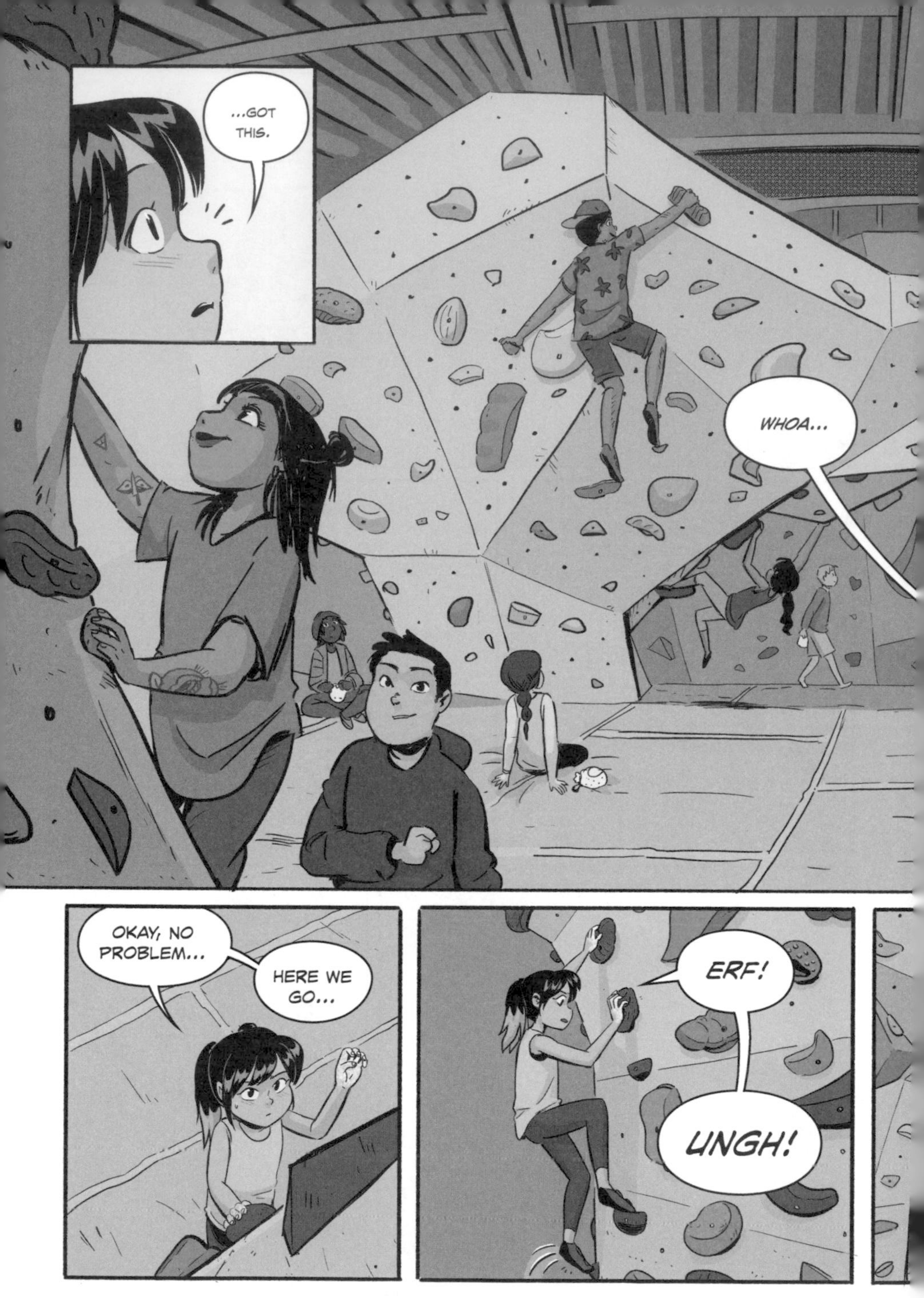
...GOT THIS.
WHOA...
OKAY, NO PROBLEM...
HERE WE GO...
ERF!
UNGH!

GULP

THAT'S *IT*, MINDY!

YOU'RE DOING *GREAT!*

BIG DEAL... *UHN!*

NOT LIKE CLIMBING IS *HARD*...

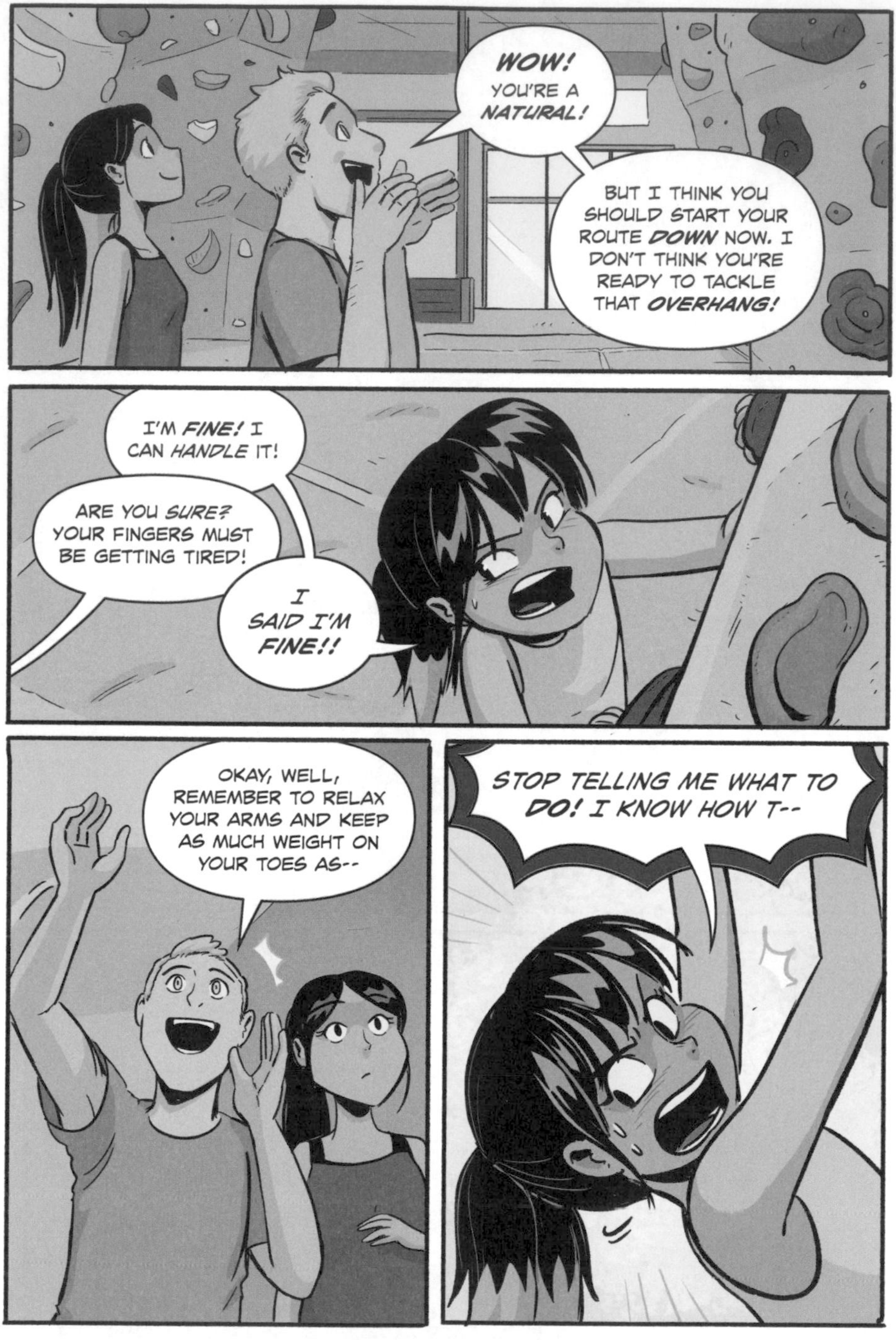
WOW! YOU'RE A NATURAL!
BUT I THINK YOU SHOULD START YOUR ROUTE DOWN NOW. I DON'T THINK YOU'RE READY TO TACKLE THAT OVERHANG!
I'M FINE! I CAN HANDLE IT!
ARE YOU SURE? YOUR FINGERS MUST BE GETTING TIRED!
I SAID I'M FINE!!
OKAY, WELL, REMEMBER TO RELAX YOUR ARMS AND KEEP AS MUCH WEIGHT ON YOUR TOES AS--
STOP TELLING ME WHAT TO DO! I KNOW HOW T--

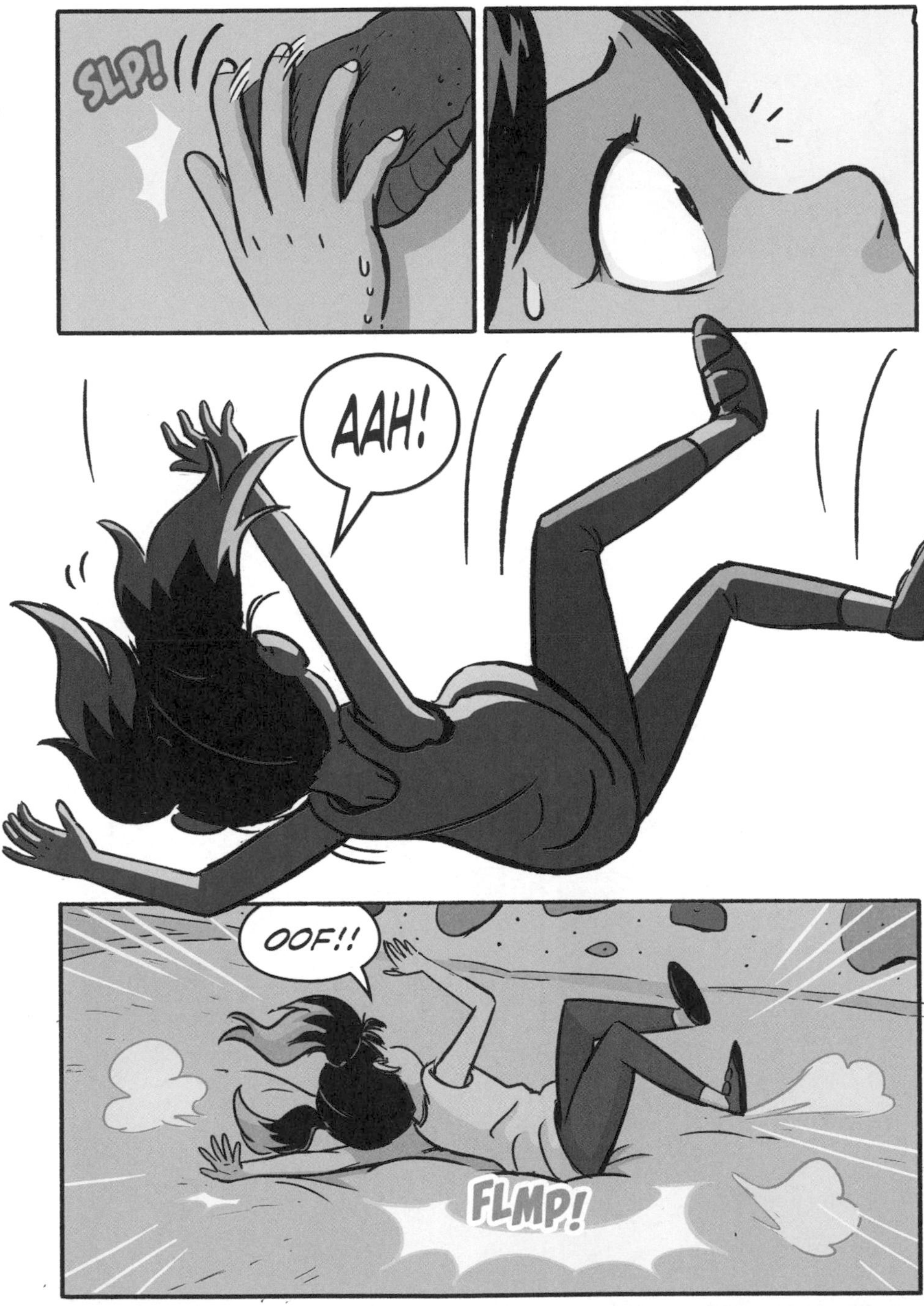
SLP!
AAH!
OOF!!
FLMP!

MINDY!

MINDY! ARE YOU OKAY?

UNH...

NO!

I *HATE* THIS STUPID PLACE!!

REALLY? THESE MATS ARE PRETTY SOFT...

WELL, OBVIOUSLY NOT SOFT *ENOUGH!* MY SHOULDER IS *KILLING ME!*

I-I'M SO SORRY. I *TRIED* TO TELL YOU--

OH, SO IT'S *MY FAULT?!*

NO! I-I DIDN'T *MEAN* THAT! I JUST...I...

IT'S OKAY, MICHAEL. I'VE SEEN HER TAKE MUCH WORSE TUMBLES OFF A *SKATEBOARD.*

I'M SURE SHE'LL BE *FINE.*

NO, I *WON'T!!* I WANT TO *GO!*

OH, MINDY, JUST WAIT...

I...

SIGH...

HAHAHA!

THAT WAS *FUN!*

WHEN'S *DINNER?* I'M *STARVING!*

I JUST WATCHED YOU EAT LIKE *HALF* THAT BOWL OF CHIPS!

I'M A *GROWING GIRL,* PRIYA.

MOM! WHEN DOES THE *PIZZA* ARRIVE??!

IN ABOUT A HALF HOUR, DEAR!

UGH! WHAT DO YOU GUYS WANT TO DO UNTIL *THEN?*

OH! MAYBE WE CAN DO SOMETHING ON OUR *PHONES?*

GROAN!

WHOA!

WHAT'S ...GOING ON?

BONK!

AH, GABBY'S JUST MAD CUZ *SHE* DOESN'T *HAVE* A PHONE.

WHY *NOT?*

MY PARENTS ARE *SO NOT COOL* ABOUT SCREEN TIME.

THEY SAY IT'LL *"ROT MY BRAIN"!*

DO *YOU* HAVE A PHONE, PRIYA?

YEAH, MY DAD JUST GOT ME ONE.

IT'S NOT GREAT, BUT I DON'T USE IT MUCH...

MINDY IS THE *REAL* SCREEN JUNKIE IN *PAWS.*

SHE RUNS OUR PICTAGRAM ACCOUNT AND EVERYTHING.

OMG, YOU HAVE A PICTAGRAM ACCOUNT FOR *PAWS?!*

WHAT'S THE *NAME* OF IT?!

YEAH!

PRETTY_AWESOME _WALKERS!

91

HAHA! WAIT, *PAWS* IS AN *ACRONYM?* WHAT DOES THE "S" EVEN *STAND* FOR?

THAT'S WHAT *I* SAID!!

OH, *WOW!* THIS IS *SO COOL!*

HAHA! LOOK AT *THIS* ONE!

OH, I *LOVE* THESE LI'L GUYS!

FOLLOW US, AND THEN MINDY CAN FOLLOW YOU *BACK!*

SWIPE

OKAY!

I'LL *TEXT* HER TO LET HER KNOW!

HAHAHA! LOOK AT THIS ONE OF *SCRAPS!*

OH MY GOODNESS! HIS LITTLE SAD *FACE!!!*

ANY REPLY FROM MINDY YET?

NO. THAT'S ODD...SHE ALWAYS TEXTS BACK IN LIKE *TEN* SECONDS.

HER PHONE IS PRACTICALLY *GLUED* TO HER HAND.

LET'S *FACECHAT* HER!

YEAH!

HUH?

BRRM

HELLO?

HI, *MINDY!!*

HI! MINDY, IT'S *US!*

UH, YEAH, I CAN *SEE* THAT.

WHERE THE HECK *ARE* YOU?!

IN MICHAEL'S CAR. WE JUST LEFT THE CLIMBING GYM.

WHY ARE YOU *CALLING?*

WE WANT YOU TO LOG IN TO THE *PAWS* PICTA ACCOUNT AND FOLLOW *HAZEL* BACK!

♪ DING-DONG ♫

HUH?

OH!! IS IT--

I THINK SO!

THAT MUST BE THE *PIZZA!*

I'LL GET IT, MOM!!

HI, THERE! YOU MUST BE HAZEL!

I'M MALCOLM-- GABBY'S DAD...

...AND I'VE GOT SOMEONE WHO'D LIKE TO *MEET* YOU!

ARF!

GASP!

THANKS, DAD! YOU'RE THE *BEST!*

YOU *BET!* IT'S MY PLEAS--

SLAM!!

--URE.

DID I HEAR THAT RIGHT? YOU'RE *GABBY'S* DAD?

95

I'M *HAZEL'S* DAD! WANT TO JOIN ME AROUND BACK IN THE GARAGE OF EXILED DADS?

?

I HAVE LEFTOVER HALLOWEEN CANDY!!

...AND SCRAPS'S OWNER SAID IT'D BE OKAY TO BRING HIM OVER FOR A VISIT!

OMG OMG OMG

SNIFF! SNUFF!

ARF!

OH!

OH, YOU LITTLE OLD *BABY* MAN!!

SO? GOOD BIRTHDAY SURPRISE?

BEST.

BIRTHDAY.

EVER!

HELLO? WHAT'S GOING *ON?* I CAN'T *SEE!*

OH, *HAHA!* I FORGOT YOU WERE STILL ON THE CALL!

SORRY, MINDY! GOTTA GO! I'LL TEXT YOU *TOMORROW!*

BEEP!

OVER THE NEXT COUPLE OF WEEKS, THINGS KEEP ON GOING PRETTY MUCH THE SAME WAY. THERE ARE A *FEW* GOOD MOMENTS-- LIKE THE NEW DOGS FITTING IN SO WELL WITH THE PACK--BUT EVERYTHING ELSE JUST GETS *WORSE.*

PRIYA GETS INTO SOME KIND OF ELITE SOCCER PROGRAM, WHICH MAKES IT *WAY* HARDER FOR HER TO KEEP UP HER *PAWS* DUTIES.

PLUS, ROXY'S OWNER HAS A SETBACK IN HER RECOVERY AND NEEDS US TO WALK ROXY MORE OFTEN! WHICH LEADS TO US BREAKING OUR *RULE* OF ONE DOG EACH...

...WITH *PREDICTABLE* RESULTS!

MEANWHILE, *HAZEL* SEEMS TO BE HAVING NO PROBLEM AT ALL FITTING IN WITH HER *OWN* NEW PACK.

IS SHE FUNNY? YEAH, SURE, I *GUESS.* NICE? UGH, *SO* NICE. *ANNOYINGLY* NICE.

BUT I WAS FRIENDS WITH GABBY AND PRIYA *FIRST!* AND NOW IT FEELS LIKE, IF THEY'RE NOT WALKING DOGGOS WITH ME, THEY'D RATHER BE HANGING OUT WITH *HAZEL!*

GABBY EVEN INVITES *HER* TO THE LOCAL *COMIC CON!* THAT USED TO BE *OUR* THING!! JUST HER AND *ME!*

AND THEN THERE'S MICHAEL. THE GUY COMES WITH US ALMOST *EVERYWHERE* NOW.

HE'S *ALWAYS* AROUND! IT'S, LIKE, *SO* CRINGE.

LIKE, DUDE--GET YOUR *OWN* LIFE!

THE ONLY UPSIDE IS THAT AT LEAST I GET TO SPEND A BIT OF TIME WITH *CHONK.*

THIS CAT IS RIDICULOUS. JUST THE BIGGEST, SOFTEST, GENTLEST FLOOF MONSTER EVER.

HOW A DORK LIKE MICHAEL ENDED UP WITH A CAT THIS GREAT IS A *MYSTERY.*

HAHA! HEY, MOM--LOOK AT *CHONK!!*

...MOM?

I FEEL LIKE EVERYWHERE I LOOK, I'M BEING *SQUEEZED OUT*.

LIKE THERE'S NO *SPACE* FOR ME ANYMORE.

IT FEELS...LIKE I'M BEING *REPLACED*.

YOINK!

HEY!! THAT'S THE LAST *DYNAMITE ROLL!!*

Kishimoto apanese Restaurant

Best Sushi Eat with your Eyes! Eat in Take out

岸本 KISHIMOTO

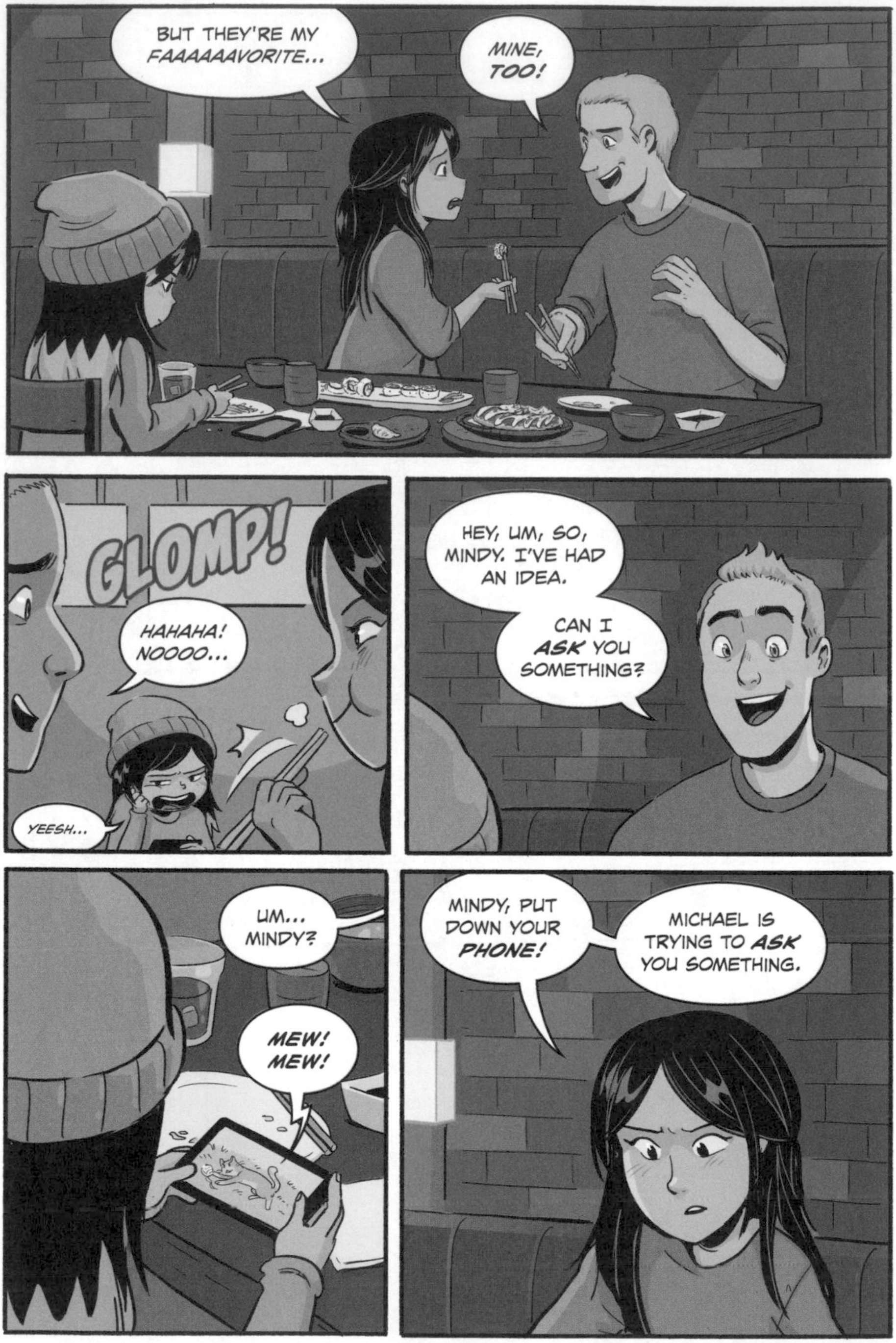
BUT THEY'RE MY FAAAAAAVORITE...
MINE, TOO!
GLOMP!
HAHAHA! NOOOO...
YEESH...
HEY, UM, SO, MINDY. I'VE HAD AN IDEA.
CAN I ASK YOU SOMETHING?
UM... MINDY?
MEW! MEW!
MINDY, PUT DOWN YOUR PHONE!
MICHAEL IS TRYING TO ASK YOU SOMETHING.

OH, SORRY.

WHAT?

WELL, UM, AS I WAS SAYING, YOUR MOM HAS TOLD ME SO MUCH ABOUT *PAWS* AND EVERYTHING YOU AND YOUR FRIENDS DO...AND, UM...

...WELL, I WAS WONDERING IF YOU GIRLS COULD WALK *CHONK* FOR ME?

CHONK?

YOU WANT TO *PAY* US.

TO WALK *CHONK*.

SURE! I MEAN, I KNOW THAT YOU MOSTLY JUST WALK DOGS, BUT I'VE BEEN WALKING CHONK FOR *YEARS!* HE *LIKES* IT!

COULD YOU JUST TAKE HIM AROUND THE BLOCK A FEW TIMES EVERY WEEK?

YOU'VE PROBABLY NOTICED--HE COULD *USE* A BIT MORE EXERCISE...

I'LL SAY.

RIGHT?

PLUS, I WORRY HE DOESN'T GET MUCH ENRICHMENT DURING THE DAYS WHEN I HAVE TO GO INTO THE OFFICE.

YEAH, I'M NOT SURE--

I-IT DOESN'T NEED TO BE EVERY *DAY* OR ANYTHING! OR EVEN FOR THAT *LONG!*

I'LL TAKE WHAT I CAN *GET.*

I JUST DON'T THINK WE CAN REALLY--

UHH...

UM...

...WELL, I, UH...

"I MEAN..."

...SURE.

YEAH, WE CAN PROBABLY DO THAT.

AH, *GREAT!*

I'VE ALREADY GOT A SPARE HOUSE KEY HERE FOR YOU SOMEWHERE...

YOU *SEE?*

I *TOLD* YOU SHE'D THINK IT WAS A GOOD IDEA!

YEP! YOU WERE *TOTALLY* RIGHT.

GREAT. JUST *GREAT.*

HOW THE *HECK* AM I SUPPOSED TO SELL THIS TO THE GIRLS?!

HAHAHA!

HEY, CHECK IT *OUT!*

LOOKS LIKE *DODY* MIGHT HAVE A NEW *BOYFRIEND!*

HEY, UM...SPEAKING OF BOYFRIENDS...YOU KNOW THAT *GUY* MY MOM HAS BEEN DATING?

OH, IS YOUR MOM *DATING A GUY?*

THIS IS THE FIRST TIME I'M HEARING ABOUT *THIS.*

I, PERSONALLY, AM *SHOCKED* AT THIS NEWS.

CAN'T BELIEVE YOU HAVEN'T *MENTIONED* IT BEFORE.

HAHA, OKAY, VERY *FUNNY.*

ANYWAY, HE'S GOT THIS MASSIVE *CAT* NAMED *CHONK,* AND, WELL...

...MICHAEL WANTS TO HIRE US TO, UM... *WALK* HIM.

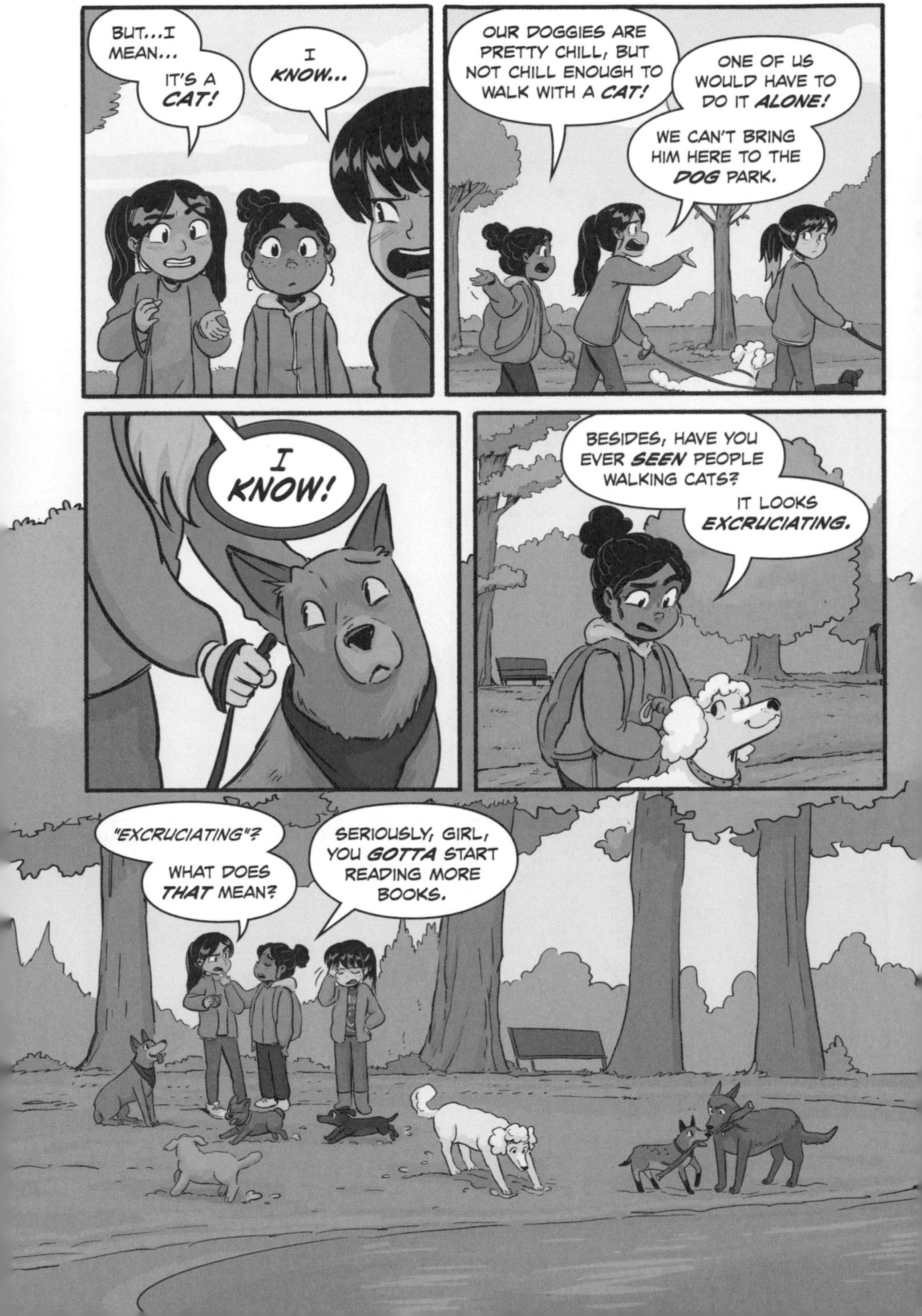
BUT...I MEAN...
IT'S A CAT!
I KNOW...
OUR DOGGIES ARE PRETTY CHILL, BUT NOT CHILL ENOUGH TO WALK WITH A CAT!
ONE OF US WOULD HAVE TO DO IT ALONE!
WE CAN'T BRING HIM HERE TO THE DOG PARK.
I KNOW!
BESIDES, HAVE YOU EVER SEEN PEOPLE WALKING CATS?
IT LOOKS EXCRUCIATING.
"EXCRUCIATING"?
WHAT DOES THAT MEAN?
SERIOUSLY, GIRL, YOU GOTTA START READING MORE BOOKS.

HA!

YOU'RE RIGHT ABOUT WALKING CATS, THOUGH. CHONK *BARELY* MOVES.

HE JUST LIKES TO SNIFF PLANTS AND EAT GRASS.

WELL...MAYBE IT'S JUST SOMETHING ONE OF US CAN DO *AFTER* WE ALL WALK THE DOGS?

THAT'D BE A LONG DAY FOR *ONE* OF US, THOUGH...

I *KNOW!* I'M *SORRY*, OKAY? IT'S TOO MUCH!

WE ALREADY HAVE SO MANY DOGS, AND NOW A *CAT?!*

ACTUALLY...

YEAH, THIS MIGHT BE A GOOD TIME TO BRING IT UP.

I TRIED TO TELL MICHAEL NO, BUT MY MOM...

YOU SHOULD HAVE SEEN THE *LOOK* SHE WAS GIVING ME!

SO, THIS MIGHT...

HEY, LISTEN, MINDY--

JUST THESE ABSOLUTE *DEATH LASERS!*

MINDY!

LISTEN!!

OKAY, JEEZ-- WHAT?!

SORRY, BUT, WELL, SO PRIYA AND I WERE TALKING WITH HAZEL AT LUNCH, AND UM, WELL...

YOU SEE, THE THING IS...WELL, IT'S FUNNY, BUT, UM...I...

WELL...AND NOW WITH THIS *CAT*, IT REALLY DOES SEEM LIKE IT'LL BE A BIG HELP, AND, UM, IT'S--

WE ASKED *HAZEL* TO JOIN *PAWS.*

SHE'S GOING TO START WITH US TOMORROW.

WH-WHAT?

WE DIDN'T *PLAN* TO ASK HER! I-IT JUST KINDA CAME UP!

AND BEFORE YOU *FREAK OUT,* JUST LOOK--WINTER SOCCER LEAGUE STARTS SOON AND I'LL NEED TO MISS EVEN MORE WALKS. YOU NEED *HELP!*

IT'LL ACTUALLY WORK OUT *GREAT,* SINCE HAZEL CAN REALLY ONLY HELP OUT A COUPLE DAYS A WEEK--

SHE HAS A LOT OF AFTER-SCHOOL STUFF--

SO SHE'LL REALLY ONLY BE PICKING UP *MY* SLACK!

BUT...

MINDY, WE THINK THIS IS A *TERRIFIC* IDEA, AND WE'RE HONESTLY NOT SURE WHY YOU'RE *AGAINST* IT.

CAN YOU *EXPLAIN* WHY YOU DON'T LIKE HER? LIKE, IS THERE SOMETHING WE'RE *MISSING?*

BECAUSE WE THINK SHE'S *REALLY NICE.*

NO, I...

...I--I JUST...

OKAY, *FINE!*

BUT IF WE'RE GOING TO DO THIS, WE NEED TO DO IT *MY* WAY.

WHAT DOES *THAT* MEAN?

HAZEL CAN JOIN *PAWS*, BUT ON... ON A TRIAL BASIS!

OKAYYY... I GUESS THAT'S FAIR--

BUT WHAT DOES THAT EVEN *MEAN*?

WELL, SHE'S GOT TO *PROVE* THAT SHE CAN HANDLE IT!

HOW'S SHE GONNA DO *THAT*?

SHE NEEDS TO START SMALL. NO BIG DOGS! NO DOGS AT *ALL*, IN FACT!

SHE'LL BE IN CHARGE OF WALKING *CHONK!*

I DON'T KNOW, MINDY...

HEY, LOOK--*YOU TWO* ASKED HER TO BE A MEMBER. I'M TRYING TO GO ALONG, BUT YOU'VE GOT TO *GIVE* ME SOMETHING HERE.

PAWS IS MY BABY, *TOO!*

IT JUST SOUNDS LIKE YOU'RE TRYING TO GET RID OF *HAZEL* AND THIS *CAT* ALL IN ONE GO.

NO! THAT'S NOT IT AT **ALL!**

(*IT TOTALLY IS THAT.*)

I--I JUST WANT TO BE SURE SHE CAN *HANDLE* SOMETHING AS SIMPLE AS A CAT BEFORE WE *TRUST* HER WITH ONE OF OUR DOGS.

HMM.

SOME OF OUR DOGS ARE PRETTY *FAST!*

EVEN *GABBY* AND I HAVE A HARD TIME KEEPING UP, AND WE DON'T USE A *WHEELCHAIR!*

HM...WELL, MAAAYBE.

I'M NOT SURE HOW WE'LL EXPLAIN THE WHOLE *TRIAL* THING TO HER, THOUGH.

JUST LEAVE IT TO *ME!*

I'LL EXPLAIN EVERYTHING TO HAZEL TOMORROW! *TRUST* ME.

THE NEXT DAY...

THIS IS *SO EXCITING!!*

I FEEL LIKE I'VE BEEN WAITING *FOREVER* TO WALK THESE DOGS WITH YOU GUYS!

WELL, WE'RE EXCITED TO *HAVE* YOU!

YEAH, I WISH WE'D ASKED YOU *SOONER.*

BUT YOU UNDERSTAND THE *DEAL,* RIGHT? THIS IS A *TRIAL* MEMBERSHIP-- YOU GOTTA START *SMALL.*

RIGHT! WITH A *CAT!* THAT'S OKAY. I THINK I CAN HANDLE THAT.

GREAT! *SEE?!*

HMM...

JUST WAIT RIGHT HERE WHILE I GO GET *CHONK*, GIRLS!

O-OKAY.

H-HAVE YOU GUYS WALKED CHONK BEFORE?

UH, NO. THIS IS THE FIRST TIME!

I GUESS IT'S KINDA LIKE A TRIAL FOR *BOTH* OF YOU!

OH. DID *YOU* HAVE TO DO A TRIAL MEMBERSHIP IN *PAWS*, TOO?

WELL, NO...BUT WE WERE THE *FOUNDERS*, SO WE WERE KINDA JUST MAKING IT UP AS WE WENT ALONG.

YEAH, WE HAD *NO* IDEA WHAT WE WERE DOING.

STILL *DON'T*, IN FACT...

OKAY, GANG!!! HERE COMES THE *KING!!*

OOF...MAYBE SKIP A *MEAL* OR TWO ONCE IN A WHILE, CHONKSTER...

OH! MY! GOSH!

HUP. DOWN YA GO, BIG GUY.

LOOK AT THE *SIZE* OF YOU, BIG BOI!

ARE WE SURE THIS IS JUST *ONE* CAT?

HERE YOU *GO*, HAZEL!

O-OKAY. GOT IT!

OKAY, LOOKS LIKE YOU'RE ALL *SET!* WE'LL BE BACK ONCE WE'VE WALKED OUR DOGS.

SHOULDN'T BE MORE THAN AN *HOUR* OR SO.

AN ...*HOUR?*

COME ON, GIRLS! LET'S GET *MOVING!*

THESE DOGS WON'T WALK *THEMSELVES!*

YOU'VE GOT MY NUMBER! JUST *TEXT* ME IF YOU NEED ANYTHING!

SEE YOU *SOON!*

O-OKAY.

BYE, GUYS.

GULP

MRR.

THIS IS *GREAT!*

THEY'RE GONNA HAVE SUCH A GOOD *TIME* TOGETHER!

YOU REALLY *THINK* SO?

OF *COURSE!*

WHAT COULD EVEN GO *WRONG?*

CHONK IS THE *CHILLEST* CAT! IT'S NOT LIKE HE'LL RUN AWAY. I DON'T EVEN THINK HE *CAN* RUN.

OKAY! LET'S SPLIT UP AND GET OUR *PUPPERS!*

I'LL SEE YOU AT THE *PARK!*

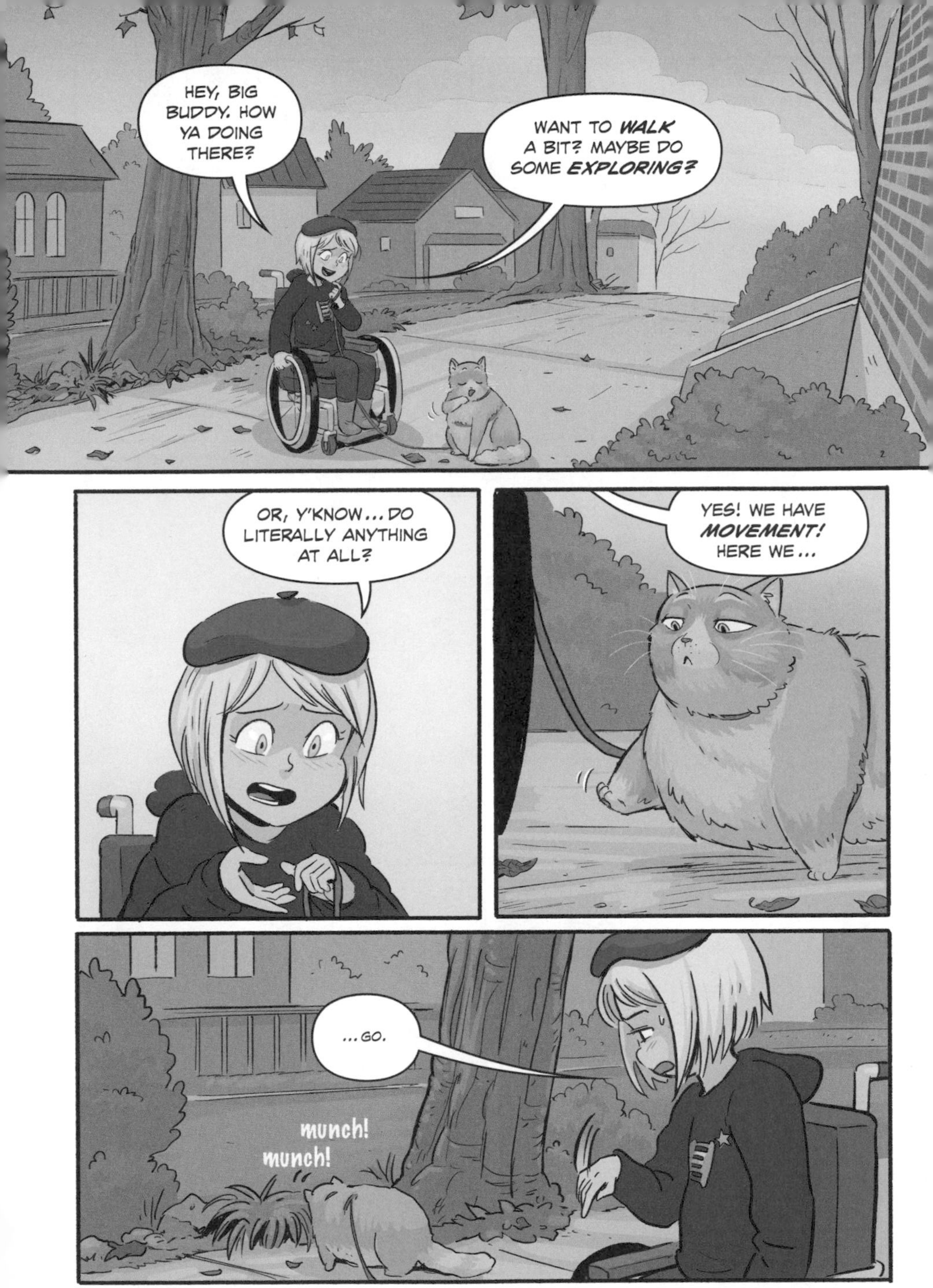
HEY, BIG BUDDY. HOW YA DOING THERE?
WANT TO *WALK* A BIT? MAYBE DO SOME *EXPLORING?*
OR, Y'KNOW... DO LITERALLY ANYTHING AT ALL?
YES! WE HAVE *MOVEMENT!* HERE WE...
...GO.
munch!
munch!

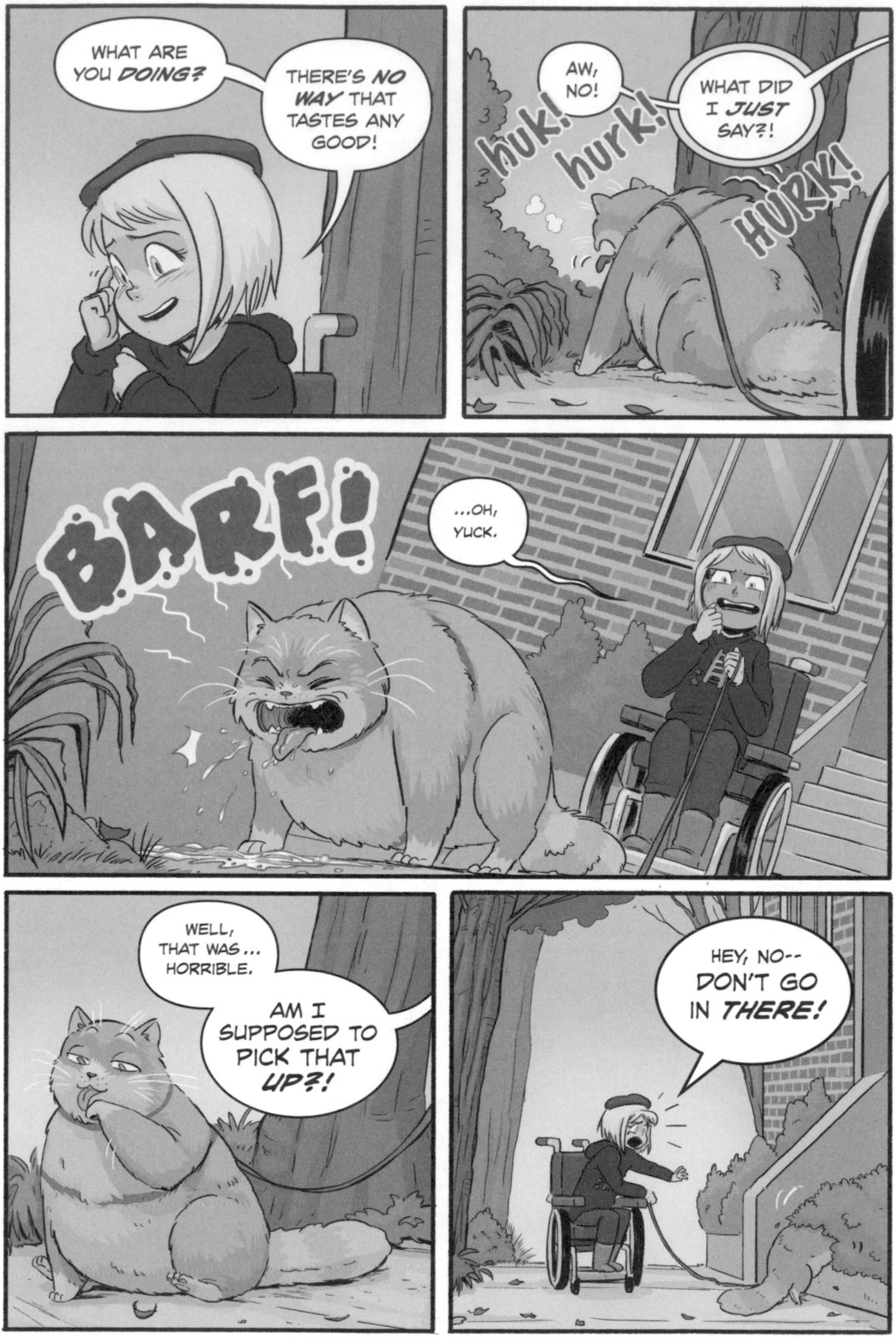
WHAT ARE YOU DOING?
THERE'S NO WAY THAT TASTES ANY GOOD!
huk! hurk!
AW, NO!
WHAT DID I JUST SAY?!
HURK!
BARF!
...OH, YUCK.
WELL, THAT WAS... HORRIBLE.
AM I SUPPOSED TO PICK THAT UP?!
HEY, NO-- DON'T GO IN THERE!

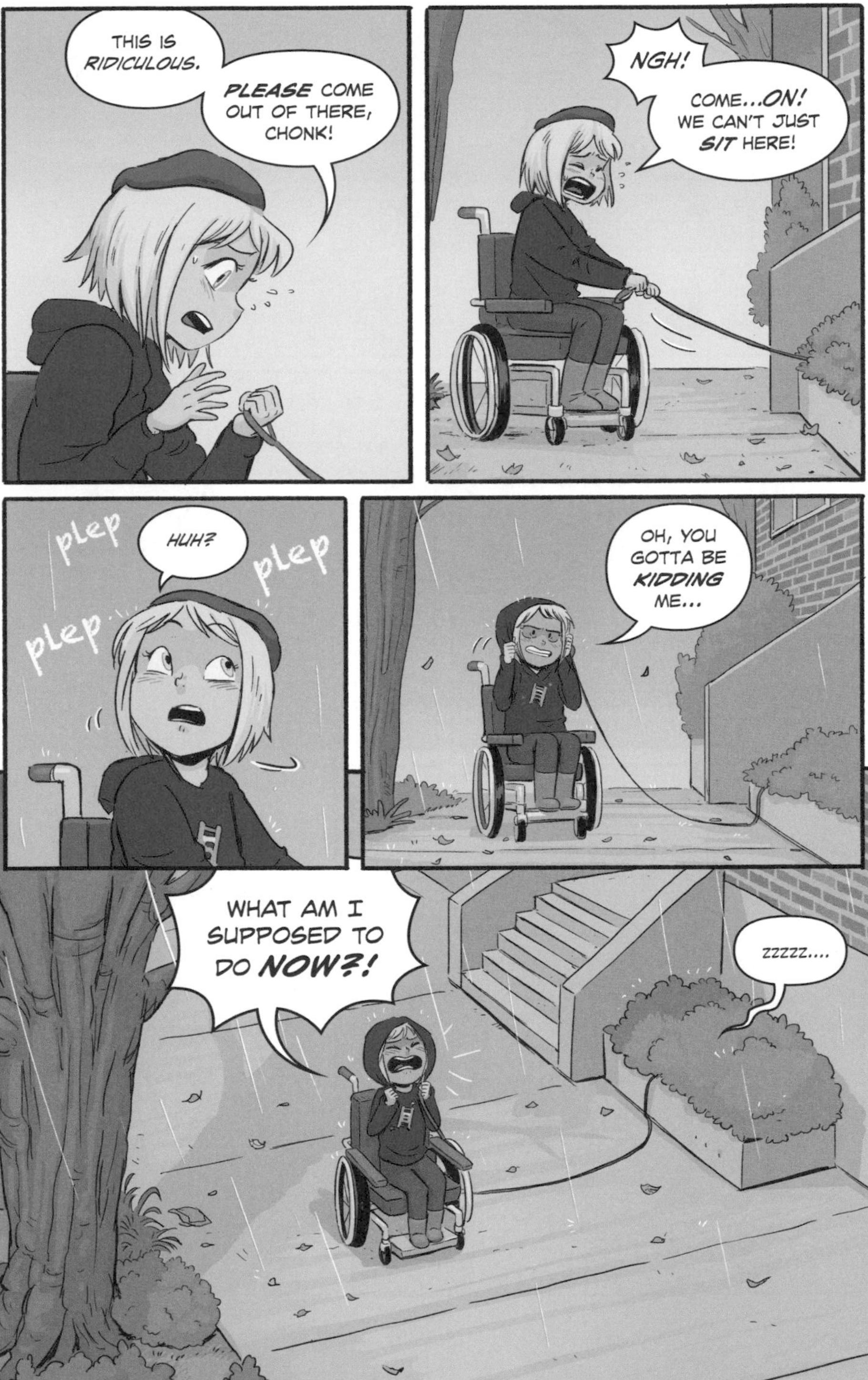
THIS IS RIDICULOUS.
PLEASE COME OUT OF THERE, CHONK!
NGH!
COME...ON! WE CAN'T JUST SIT HERE!
plep
HUH?
plep
plep
OH, YOU GOTTA BE KIDDING ME...
WHAT AM I SUPPOSED TO DO NOW?!
ZZZZZ....

MUCH LATER...

I DON'T SEE WHAT THE BIG *HURRY* IS.

I STILL SAY WE SHOULD DROP YOUR DOGS OFF *TOO* BEFORE MEETING BACK UP WITH HAZEL.

NO *WAY!* WE'VE BEEN GONE TOO *LONG* AS IT IS.

DO YOU THINK SHE'S DOING OKAY?

MAYBE WE SHOULD HAVE GONE BACK TO *CHECK* ON HER WHEN IT STARTED *DRIZZLING.*

I TEXTED HER A COUPLE TIMES, BUT SHE DIDN'T *ANSWER.*

TRUST ME! SHE'LL BE *FINE!* THIS IS A *PERFECT* ARRANGEMENT.

MICHAEL GETS HIS *CAT* WALKED, HAZEL GETS TO JOIN *PAWS,* AND *WE* GET TO STAY TOGETHER!

IT'S *GENIUS!*

MINDY, THAT'S NOT--

OH, THERE SHE *IS!*

HEY, HAZEL! HOW WAS *THAT*?

DID YOU AND *CHONK* HAVE A...

...A...

HAZEL?

WH-WHAT'S *WRONG*?

WHAT'S WRONG? WHAT'S *WRONG*?!

YOU LEAVE ME HERE, *ALONE,* IN THE *RAIN,* WITH A CAT THAT HAS *NO* INTEREST IN WALKING, FOR OVER AN *HOUR*!

AND YOU ASK ME *WHAT'S WRONG*?!

HERE! TAKE THIS STUPID LEASH!

HEY!

I'M GOING HOME!!

OH, JEEZ! COME ON, CHONK!

GET OUT OF THERE!

HAZEL, WAIT!

UNF! LET'S GO, BIG FELLA!

!

SLAM!

MRAR?

HAZEL! CAN YOU JUST HOLD UP?

WE DIDN'T *MEAN* ANYTHING BY IT! WE JUST THOUGHT--

OH, I THINK I KNOW *EXACTLY* WHAT YOU MEANT BY IT!

YOU MEANT TO GIVE ME THE BORING, *EASY* JOB! YOU MEANT TO *CUT ME OUT!*

BECAUSE YOU DIDN'T THINK I COULD *HANDLE* WALKING A *DOG!*

NO! W-WE JUST--

THAT'S NOT IT AT *ALL!*

OH, *REALLY?!*

YOU CAN HONESTLY TELL ME THAT *NONE* OF YOU SAID, "HEY LET'S GIVE THE MASSIVE LAZY CAT TO HAZEL BECAUSE HE *BARELY MOVES* AND SHE'S IN A *WHEELCHAIR"?*

NOT *ONE* OF YOU SAID THAT?

UH... WELL... I *MIGHT* HAVE SAID--

I *KNEW* IT!

YOU *NEVER* LIKED ME! RIGHT FROM THE DAY I JOINED YOUR CLASS, YOU'VE BEEN LOOKING FOR A WAY TO CUT ME OUT AND, A-AND...*EXCLUDE* ME!!

AND SO YOU USED THE FACT THAT I USE A *WHEELCHAIR AGAINST* ME! TO GET RID OF ME! IT'S *AWFUL!*

AND YOU TWO WENT RIGHT *ALONG* WITH IT! I THOUGHT YOU WERE *NICE!*

BUT YOU'RE *NOT!* YOU'RE JUST LIKE *HER!*

WELL, *FORGET* YOU!

I DON'T WANT TO BE IN YOUR *STUPID CLUB* ANYWAY!

HAZEL, WAIT--

LEAVE ME *ALONE!*

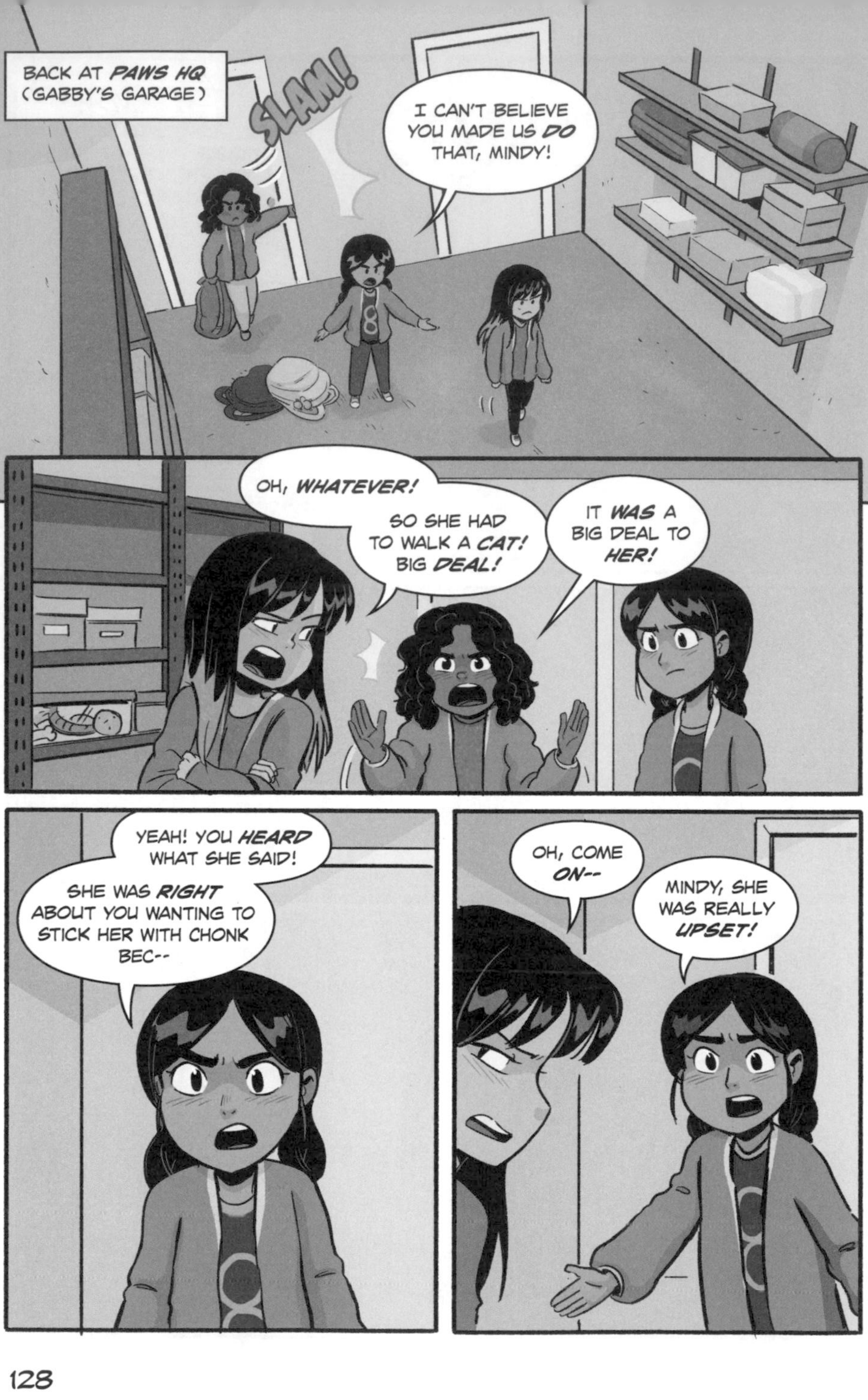
BACK AT PAWS HQ (GABBY'S GARAGE)
SLAM!
I CAN'T BELIEVE YOU MADE US DO THAT, MINDY!
OH, WHATEVER!
SO SHE HAD TO WALK A CAT! BIG DEAL!
IT WAS A BIG DEAL TO HER!
YEAH! YOU HEARD WHAT SHE SAID!
SHE WAS RIGHT ABOUT YOU WANTING TO STICK HER WITH CHONK BEC--
OH, COME ON--
MINDY, SHE WAS REALLY UPSET!

WE NEED TO *APOLOGIZE* TO HER!

THE WAY WE-- *YOU*--HAVE BEEN TREATING HER--

I KNOW! *OKAY?!*

I KNOW!

HAZEL IS *GREAT* AND SWEET AND I'M JUST A *JERK*, RIGHT?!

SO GO AHEAD AND *REPLACE* ME! SEE IF I CARE!

REPLACE YOU?

WHAT ARE YOU *TALKING* ABOUT?

OH, COME *ON!* IT'S SO *OBVIOUS!*

FIRST IT WAS MY *MOM*, AND NOW IT'S *YOU TWO!*

EVER SINCE HAZEL SHOWED UP, YOU GUYS HAVE BEEN ALL *OVER* HER!

HAZEL *THIS!*

HAZEL *THAT!*

WE WERE JUST BEING *NICE!*

OH, *RIGHT!*

I DON'T EVEN KNOW WHAT'S GOTTEN *INTO* YOU LATELY!

YOU USED TO BE NICE! *YOU* USED TO BE THE *FIRST* ONE TO GO UP TO THE NEW KID AND--

SO NOW I'M NOT *NICE?!*

NOT LATELY, NO!

TO BE PERFECTLY HONEST, LATELY YOU'VE BEEN REALLY *MEAN.*

I...

FINE, THEN! *WHATEVER!* HERE!

TAKE THIS *STUPID* JACKET AND GIVE IT TO *HAZEL,* THEN!

AARG!

MINDY, *NO* ONE WANTS YOU TO--

WHATEVER!

I'M *LEAVING!!*

MINDY, *WAIT--*

SLAM!!

MINDY!!!

131

HEY, MISTER CHONKY BUTT! I'M HO--

HEY, WHY ISN'T THE *DOOR* LOCKED?

OH, *HEY,* BIG GUY! WHAT'S GOING ON *HERE?*

MRR.

I'M *SORRY* ABOUT THAT, BUDDY.

LET'S GET YOU OUT OF THERE...

SNIFF!

♪ BRRING ♪

HEY, HANDSOME!

HEY, YOURSELF, PRETTY LADY. IS MINDY WITH YOU, BY CHANCE?

SHE'S NOT ANSWERING MY *TEXTS*.

NO, SHE SHOULD BE AT *HOME* BY NOW. I'M JUST HEADED THERE NOW.

WHAT'S *UP?*

OH, WELL, I'M SURE IT'S NOTHING--*I'M NOT UPSET OR ANYTHING*--BUT, UM...

MICHAEL, WHAT *IS* IT?

WELL, WHEN I GOT HOME, MY FRONT DOOR WAS *UNLOCKED* AND CHONK WAS STILL IN HIS HARNESS.

OH MY *GOSH!*

YEAH, SO I'M JUST WONDERING IF EVERYTHING IS OKAY WITH MINDY; OR IF SOMETHING *HAPPENED.*

MICHAEL, I AM *SO* SORRY. I'M JUST OUTSIDE MY PLACE NOW.

I'LL GET TO THE BOTTOM OF THIS AND CALL YOU *RIGHT* BACK!

CLIK!

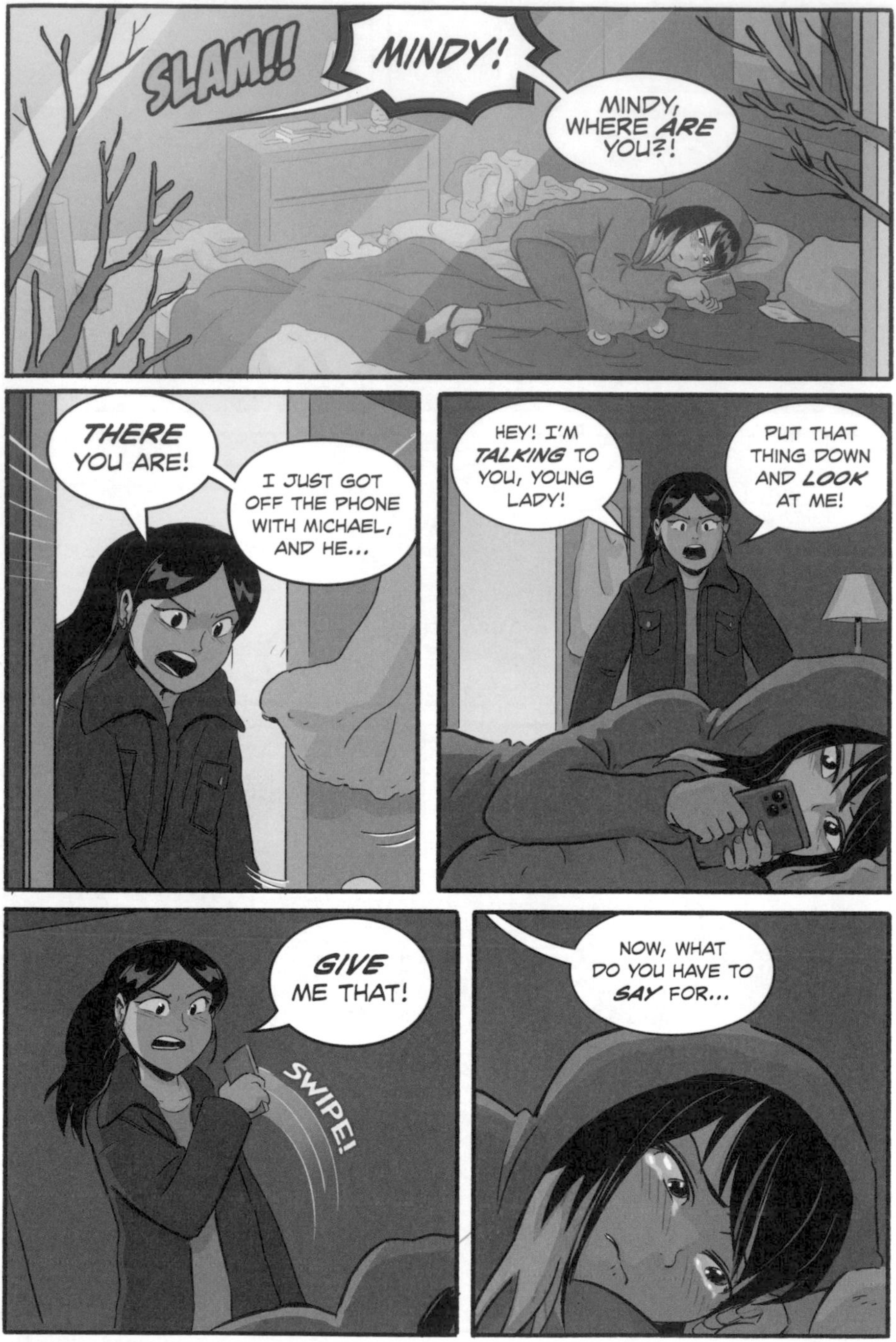
SLAM!!
MINDY!
MINDY, WHERE ARE YOU?!
THERE YOU ARE!
I JUST GOT OFF THE PHONE WITH MICHAEL, AND HE...
HEY! I'M TALKING TO YOU, YOUNG LADY!
PUT THAT THING DOWN AND LOOK AT ME!
GIVE ME THAT!
SWIPE!
NOW, WHAT DO YOU HAVE TO SAY FOR...

OH!

MINDY, WHAT'S WRONG?

DID SOMETHING *HAPPEN?*

NO.

MINDY... PLEASE. IF SOMETHING HAPPENED, I NEED TO *KNOW.*

IT'S NOTHING. I'M *FINE.*

MINDY... *TALK* TO ME. *PLEASE.*

I HAD A *FIGHT* WITH GABBY AND PRIYA, *OKAY?!*

IT'S THIS *NEW* GIRL, HAZEL! GABBY AND PRIYA WANT HER TO JOIN *PAWS* AND I *DON'T,* AND WE HAD A BIG *FIGHT* BECAUSE THEY SAID I WAS BEING *MEAN*--

BUT I *WASN'T!* OR AT LEAST I WASN'T *TRYING* TO!

I JUST DIDN'T WANT TO LET HER *IN!*

EVERYTHING WAS ALREADY *PERFECT* THE WAY IT WAS AND I DON'T WANT IT TO *CHANGE!*

AHH...

SNIFF

HEY, Y'KNOW HOW THERE ARE QUOTES BY CHARLOTTE BRONTÉ POSTED ALL AROUND YOUR SCHOOL?

NO. WHO?

CHARLOTTE BRONTË! THE WRITER YOUR SCHOOL IS *NAMED* AFTER!

OH. OKAY. ANYWAY, WHAT QUOTES?

WHAT DO YOU *MEAN*, "WHAT QUOTES"? YOU'VE NEVER SEEN THE *SIGNS* ALL OVER YOUR SCHOOL WITH QUOTES BY BRONTÉ?

NO.

THEY'RE *EVERYWHERE.* YOU'VE BEEN GOING TO BRONTÉ FOR *SEVEN YEARS!*

I HAVEN'T *SEEN* THEM, OKAY?!

HHH...

KIDS...

"OKAY, WELL, *ANYWAY,* THERE ARE PLAQUES UP ALL OVER YOUR SCHOOL WITH BRONTË QUOTES...

...AND THE ONE I LIKE THE MOST IS THE ONE WHEN YOU FIRST COME IN, BY THE GYM.

IT SAYS *'HAPPINESS QUITE UNSHARED CAN SCARCELY BE CALLED HAPPINESS.'"*

'Happiness quite
unshared can scarcely
be called happiness.'
—Charlotte Brontë

WHAT THE HECK DOES *THAT* MEAN?

IT MEANS WE NEED TO *SHARE!*

IT MEANS THAT SHARING DOESN'T *TAKE AWAY* FROM YOUR HAPPINESS...

IT'S WHAT MAKES HAPPINESS *POSSIBLE!*

OKAYYY...

SIGH

LOOK, LIFE...

LIFE IS...

I...

MOM?

SOMETIMES PEOPLE JUST...COME INTO YOUR LIFE, OKAY?

AND YOU CAN'T ALWAYS PREDICT OR *CONTROL* WHEN THAT HAPPENS.

AND MAYBE YOU DIDN'T EVEN KNOW THAT THEY WERE SOMEONE YOU WERE LOOKING FOR...

BUT THERE THEY *ARE*, ALL THE SUDDEN.

AND IT CAN BE HARD TO *MAKE SPACE* FOR THEM, MAYBE BECAUSE YOUR LIFE IS ALREADY SO FULL AND BUSY...

OR MAYBE JUST BECAUSE YOU LIKE THINGS THE WAY THAT THEY *ARE*.

AND, YEAH, SOMETIMES IT MEANS WE HAVE TO *CHANGE* THE WAY WE *DO* THINGS, BECAUSE THE WAY WE'RE USED TO DOING THINGS DOESN'T *WORK* FOR OTHERS THE WAY THAT IT WORKS FOR US.

140

BUT HERE'S THE THING, KIDDO--SOME PEOPLE ARE *WORTH* THE EFFORT.

BECAUSE IF YOU SHARE YOUR HAPPINESS WITH THEM, THEY'LL *MAKE IT BETTER.*

AND...AND IF YOU PUSH THEM *AWAY,* SOME OF THE HAPPINESS YOU WERE TRYING *SO HARD* TO KEEP TO YOURSELF...

MIGHT *LEAVE* WITH THEM, TOO.

AND WHAT YOU'LL BE *LEFT* WITH WILL BE EMPTIER AND...*LONELIER* THAN WHAT YOU STARTED OUT WITH.

...

YOU'RE NOT JUST TALKING ABOUT *PAWS,* ARE YOU?

THIS IS ABOUT *MICHAEL,* ISN'T IT?

SNIFF

MAAAAYBE...

PRETTY *SNEAKY,* MOM.

HA, THANKS. I'M *VERY* CLEVER.

SO...YOU REALLY *LIKE* HIM, HUH?

YEAH, SWEETIE. I *REALLY* DO.

UHHH, AND I'VE BEEN SO *AWFUL* TO HIM!

FLOP!

HEY, WELL, THE FACT THAT HE'S STUCK AROUND DESPITE YOU ACTING LIKE A *TROLL* IS ONE OF THE THINGS I *LIKE* ABOUT HIM.

I THINK HE MIGHT BE A *KEEPER.*

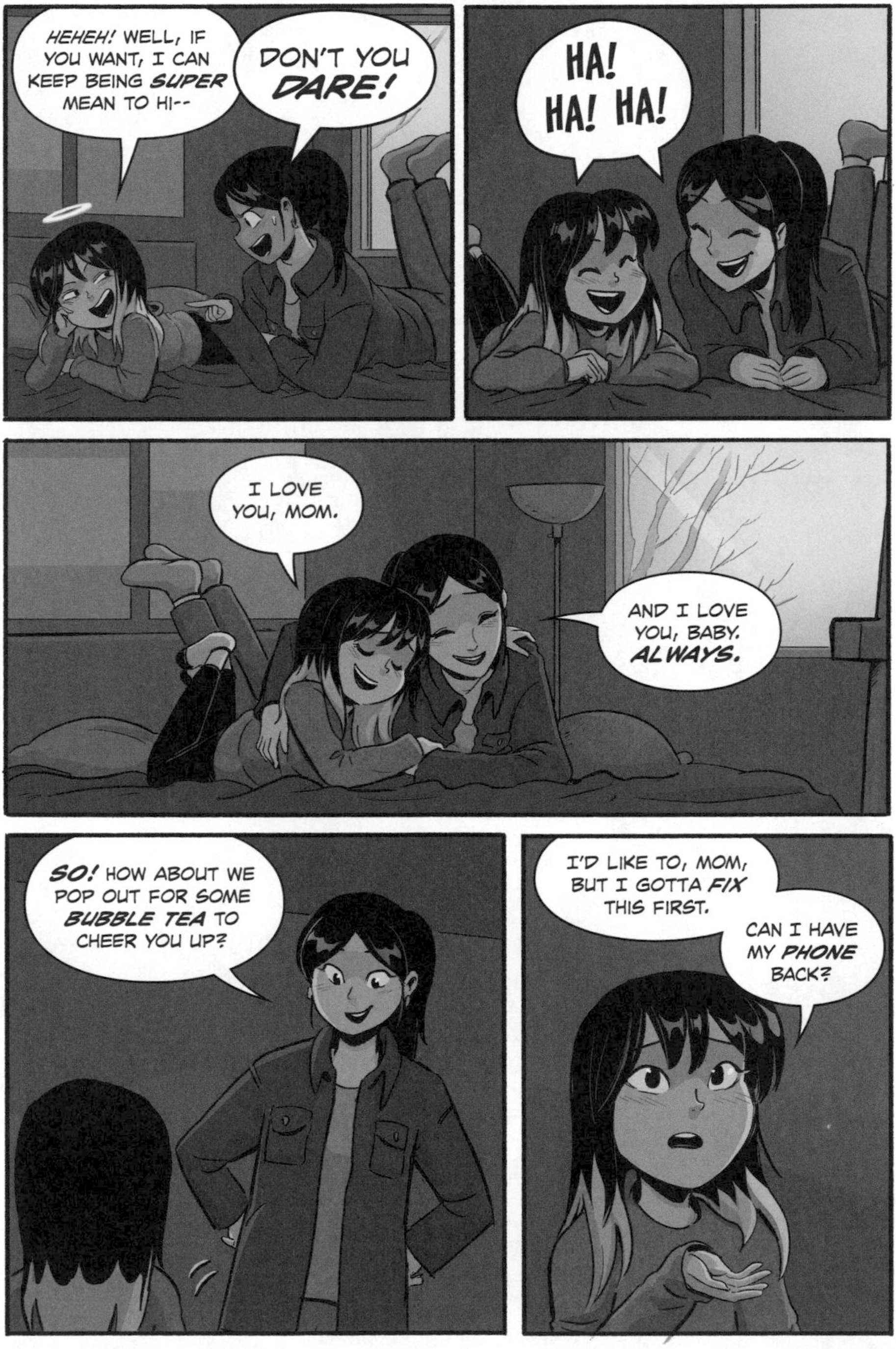
HEHEH! WELL, IF YOU WANT, I CAN KEEP BEING SUPER MEAN TO HI--
DON'T YOU DARE!
HA! HA! HA!
I LOVE YOU, MOM.
AND I LOVE YOU, BABY. ALWAYS.
SO! HOW ABOUT WE POP OUT FOR SOME BUBBLE TEA TO CHEER YOU UP?
I'D LIKE TO, MOM, BUT I GOTTA FIX THIS FIRST.
CAN I HAVE MY PHONE BACK?

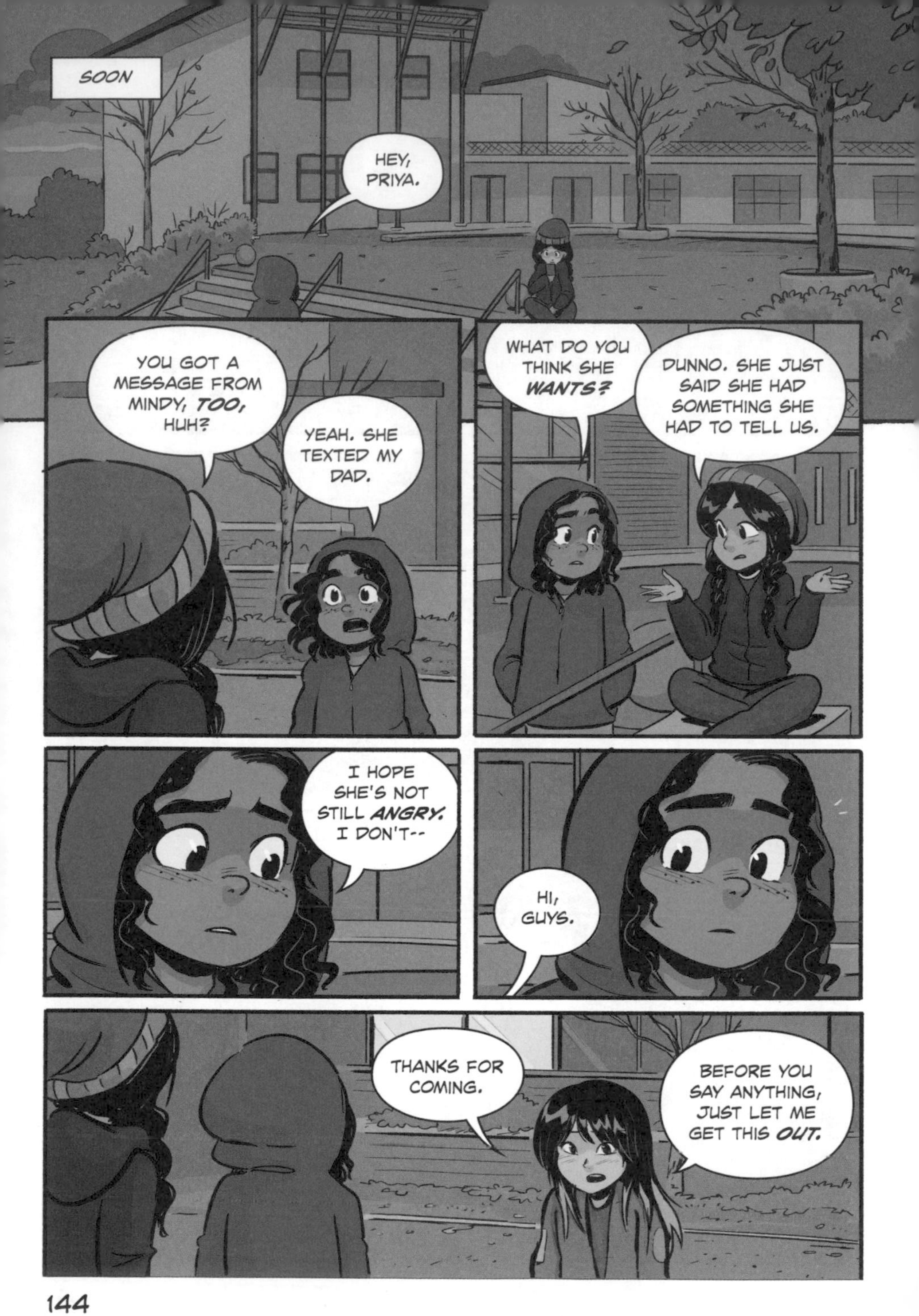
SOON
HEY, PRIYA.
YOU GOT A MESSAGE FROM MINDY, TOO, HUH?
YEAH. SHE TEXTED MY DAD.
WHAT DO YOU THINK SHE WANTS?
DUNNO. SHE JUST SAID SHE HAD SOMETHING SHE HAD TO TELL US.
I HOPE SHE'S NOT STILL ANGRY. I DON'T--
HI, GUYS.
THANKS FOR COMING.
BEFORE YOU SAY ANYTHING, JUST LET ME GET THIS OUT.

I...I KNOW THAT I'VE BEEN HARD TO BE AROUND LATELY--

REALLY HARD.

YEAH ... *REALLY* HARD. I KNOW. I WAS JUST...HAVING A HARD TIME ACCEPTING SOME ... CHANGES.

ANYWAY, IT DOESN'T *MATTER.*

I'M NOT HERE TO MAKE *EXCUSES.*

THE POINT IS THAT I'M SORRY.

I'M *REALLY* SORRY.

BUT AS MUCH AS I NEED TO MAKE IT UP TO *YOU* GUYS...

THERE'S SOME SERIOUS *PAWS* BUSINESS THAT WE NEED TO TAKE CARE OF *FIRST.*

I MEAN...THAT IS, IF YOU GUYS WILL STILL HAVE ME...

BECAUSE I... I'D UNDERSTAND IF...IF...

UGH!

ARE WE DOING *THIS* AGAIN?

HUH?

THIS WHOLE "DO YOU WANT ME IN *PAWS*" THING!

MINDY, NO ONE IS KICKING YOU OUT OF *PAWS* OR *REPLACING* YOU!

YOU'RE OUR *BEST* FRIEND!

I'M SORRY WE ARGUED, BUT YOU WERE BEING A *JERK*, AND I GUESS...

I GUESS I WAS ALSO MAD AT *MYSELF* FOR GOING ALONG WITH YOUR IDEA.

BUT WE'RE *FRIENDS*.

AND FRIENDS *WORK THINGS OUT*.

THANKS, GUYS.

OW...

CAN WE POP OVER TO YOUR GARAGE FOR A SECOND? I NEED TO *GRAB* SOMETHING.

OF *COURSE!* OUR GARAGE IS *PAWS* HEADQUARTERS, AFTER ALL!

HEH HEH.

UHH...

I...UH...I WASN'T EAVESDROPPING!

I WAS JUST, UM, OUT FOR AN EVENING *STROLL!*

YEP, JUST STRETCHING THE OLD *LEGS!* GET THE BLOOD PUMPING. TAKING IN SOME FRESH FALL AIR! AHHH! *INVIGORATING!*

WELP...

BYE!

SIGH

COME ON...

HAZEL? CAN I GET YOU ANYTHING?

NAH, THANKS, MOM. I'M GOOD.

DID YOU WANT TO TALK ABOUT IT SOME MORE?

WHAT ELSE IS THERE TO SAY?

OKAY, SWEETIE. WELL, I'M RIGHT HERE, IF YOU CHANGE YOUR MIND.

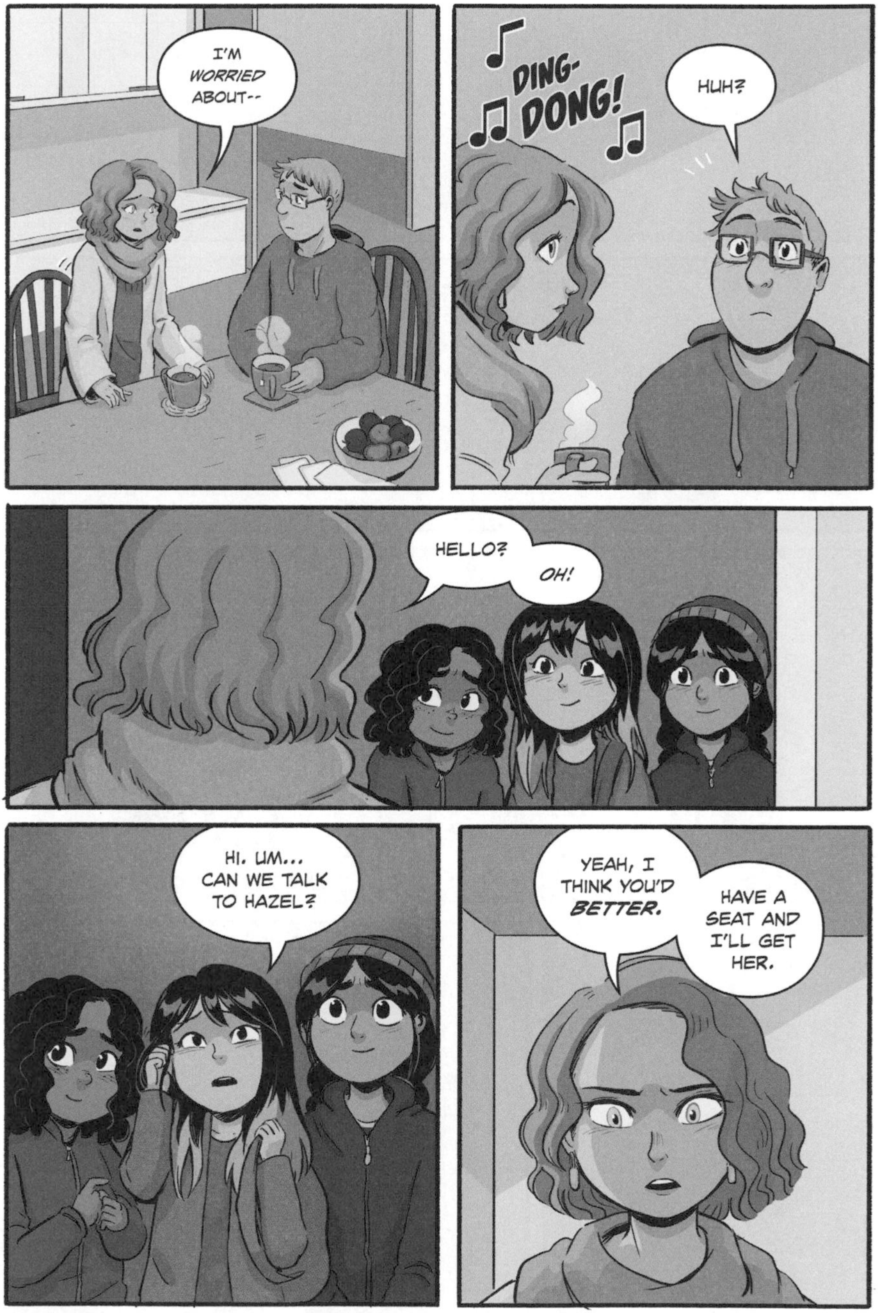
I'M *WORRIED* ABOUT--
DING-DONG!
HUH?
HELLO?
OH!
HI. UM... CAN WE TALK TO HAZEL?
YEAH, I THINK YOU'D ***BETTER.***
HAVE A SEAT AND I'LL GET HER.

HEY.

HI!

HI, HAZEL!

WHAT ARE YOU *DOING* HERE?

WE'RE HERE BECAUSE WE--NO, *I*--NEED TO TALK TO YOU, AND I WANT TO DO IT FACE-TO-FACE, NOT JUST BY TEXT.

OKAY...

HAZEL, I'M *REALLY SORRY.*

YOU *ARE?*

YES! I FEEL *TERRIBLE.* I NEVER SHOULD HAVE INSISTED THAT YOU BE LEFT BEHIND TO WALK CHONK ON YOUR *OWN.*

THAT WAS THOUGHTLESS, AND...MEAN.

THEN WHY DID YOU *DO* IT?

I JUST...I WAS BEING *SELFISH,* I GUESS.

AND...SCARED. SCARED THAT LETTING YOU IN WOULD MEAN *LOSING* STUFF I CARE ABOUT.

PAWS...

AND MY FRIENDS.

THAT'S WHY I WAS ALWAYS SHUTTING YOU *OUT.* I GUESS I JUST DIDN'T WANT TO GET TO *KNOW* YOU.

DIDN'T REALLY EVEN WANT TO GIVE YOU A *CHANCE.*

I WAS JUST HAPPY THE WAY THINGS *WERE.*

IT WAS *WRONG.*

AND...I'M *SORRY.*

SO...IT'S NOT JUST THAT I...USE A *WHEELCHAIR?*

NO! I *SWEAR!*

I JUST...I JUST DIDN'T WANT *ANYONE* BUTTING IN ON *PAWS.*

HAZEL, I AM *SO* SORRY THAT I MADE YOU FEEL LIKE THAT.

I-IT'S OKAY...

IT'S *NOT!*

YOU WERE *RIGHT* WHEN YOU GUESSED THAT I MENTIONED YOUR WHEELCHAIR TO CONVINCE GABBY AND PRIYA TO *LEAVE* YOU WITH CHONK.

THAT WAS ...*AWFUL.*

I FEEL TERRIBLE, AND...AND I HOPE YOU CAN *FORGIVE* ME.

152

A-AND I KNOW IT'S EASY TO *SAY* THAT I'M SORRY--

SO I THOUGHT MAYBE I COULD *SHOW* YOU INSTEAD.

SNIFF

I...I'M SORRY I DIDN'T COME TO YOUR BIRTHDAY PARTY, BUT...I GOT YOU THIS.

WHAT? HOW DID YOU MAKE ME THIS SO *QUICKLY?!*

WELL, ACTUALLY... THAT'S MY *OWN* JACKET.

BUT I WANT *YOU* TO HAVE IT!

AT LEAST FOR NOW!

JUST UNTIL WE CAN ORDER YOU YOUR *OWN!*

HAZEL, WE REALLY, *REALLY* WANT YOU TO JOIN *PAWS.*

WE'RE HAVING A CLUB MEETING AT LUNCHTIME ON SATURDAY TO WORK OUT SCHEDULES AND STUFF...

AND WE'D LIKE YOU TO *BE* THERE!

PLUS, IT'S A *CATERED* EVENT!

WE'RE DIPPING INTO THE CLUB FUNDS TO BUY *BANH MI*!

I...DON'T KNOW WHAT THAT IS.

WHAT?!

THEY'RE THESE VIETNAMESE SANDWICHES ON LIKE A *BAGUETTE* AND THEY PUT THESE SWEET LITTLE *PICKLES* IN THERE AND BUTTER AND I LIKE MINE WITH THIS SWEET CRISPY TOFU AND THE BREAD IS SO *CRUNCHY* BUT ALSO *SOFT*...

AND--AND...

UM.

HA! HA!

HA!

SORRY.

HA!

HA!

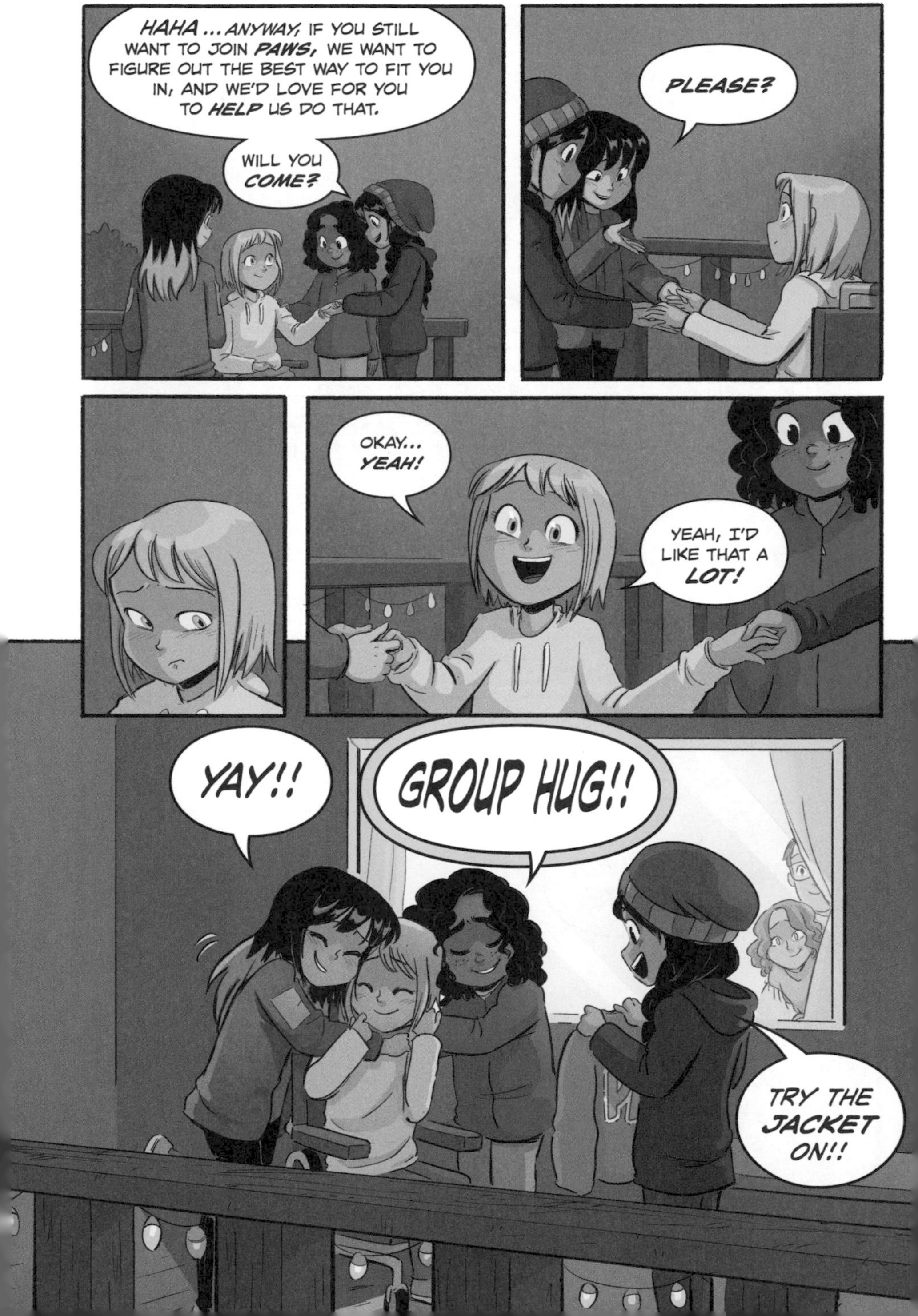
HAHA ... ANYWAY, IF YOU STILL WANT TO JOIN PAWS, WE WANT TO FIGURE OUT THE BEST WAY TO FIT YOU IN, AND WE'D LOVE FOR YOU TO HELP US DO THAT.
WILL YOU COME?
PLEASE?
OKAY... YEAH!
YEAH, I'D LIKE THAT A LOT!
YAY!!
GROUP HUG!!
TRY THE JACKET ON!!

ONCE WE ALL PUT OUR HEADS TOGETHER, WORKING OUT HOW TO INCLUDE HAZEL IN PAWS IS *WAY* SIMPLER THAN I'D THOUGHT!

I CAN TELL FROM THE FIRST DAY HOW MUCH HELP SHE'LL BE AT COVERING FOR PRIYA AND HELPING US STAY *ORGANIZED!*

THE GIRL IS A *WIZARD* WITH A TIMETABLE!

· G
· M
· P
· H

M T W T F S S

Pickles   Roxy   Dody
C. Wags   Carl   Chonk
Scraps   Champion Jack

LADIES!

LUNCH TIME!

(PLUS, SHE LIKES GABBY'S TASTE IN *SNACKS*, WHICH IS A *MUST* FOR BEING A MEMBER OF *PAWS*, LOL.)

HAVING HAZEL ON THE TEAM MEANS WE CAN GO BACK TO FOLLOWING OUR *RULE* OF ONE DOG PER DOG WALKER.

AND THE CHANGES WE NEED TO MAKE ARE HONESTLY *NO PROBLEM*.

THE MAIN THING IS THAT HAZEL'S PARENTS DON'T WANT HER WALKING HER DOG ALONE, WHICH I *TOTALLY* GET.

MOST OF OUR DOGS DON'T EVEN LIVE IN WHEELCHAIR-ACCESSIBLE HOUSING, SO IT MAKES SENSE TO STICK TOGETHER, ANYWAY!

HIYA, PICKLES!!

LET'S GO GET *SCRAPS!*

IT'S LIKE MY MOM SAID--SOMETIMES YOU GOTTA CHANGE THE WAY YOU **DO** STUFF SO THAT IT WORKS FOR **OTHER** PEOPLE.

(OR SOMETHING LIKE THAT-- I'M NOT...A GREAT LISTENER.)

HEY, GUYS!

AT ANY RATE, THE POINT IS THAT MAKING THOSE CHANGES IS **WORTH** IT FOR SOMEBODY LIKE HAZEL.

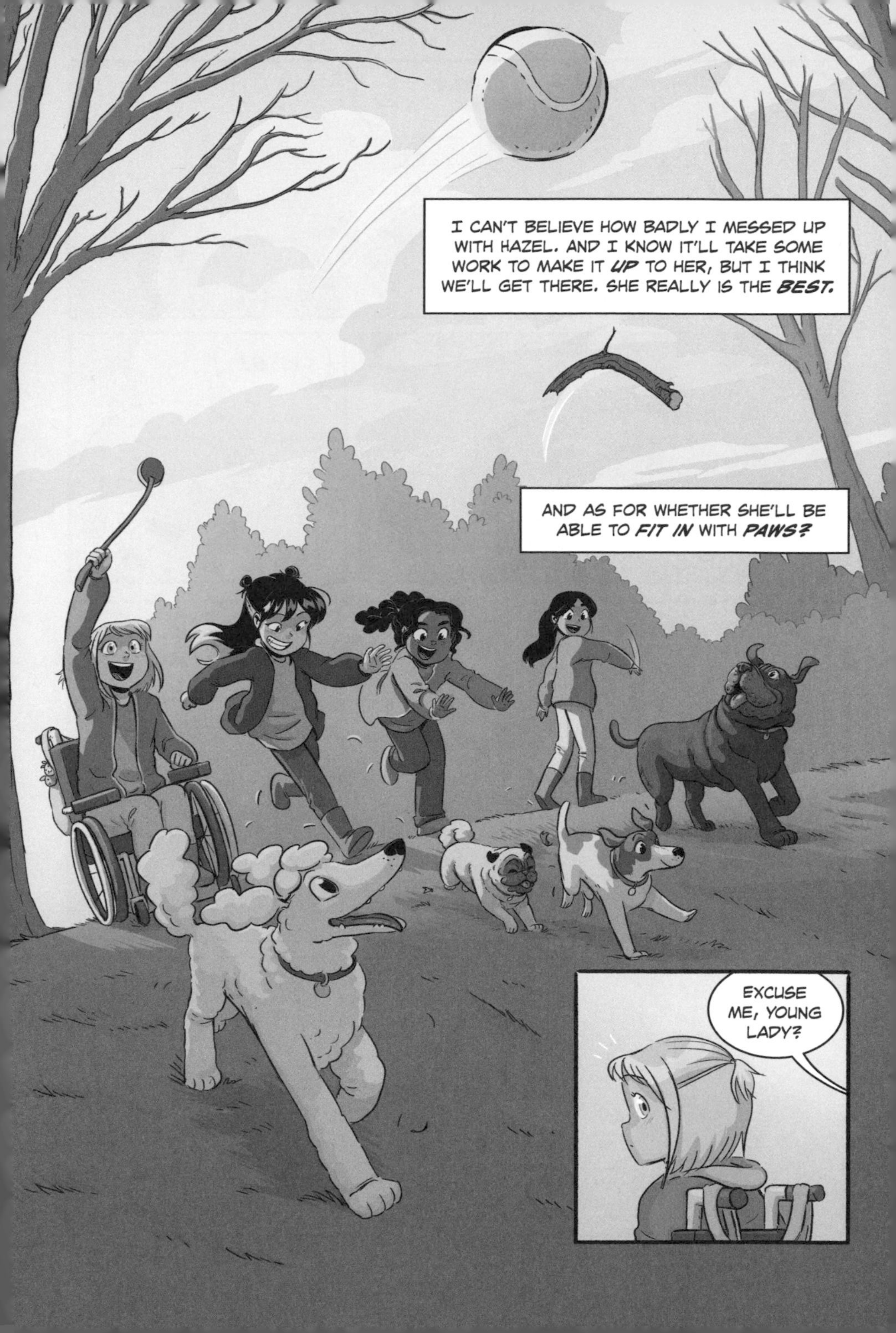
I CAN'T BELIEVE HOW BADLY I MESSED UP WITH HAZEL. AND I KNOW IT'LL TAKE SOME WORK TO MAKE IT *UP* TO HER, BUT I THINK WE'LL GET THERE. SHE REALLY IS THE ***BEST.***
AND AS FOR WHETHER SHE'LL BE ABLE TO ***FIT IN*** WITH ***PAWS?***
EXCUSE ME, YOUNG LADY?

OH! *HI!* YES?

ARE YOU GIRLS *DOG WALKERS?*

THIS LITTLE GUY IS *EXHAUSTING.*

I COULD *USE* SOME HELP!

OH, UHH...

YES!

YES, WE *ARE!*

HANG ON--I THINK WE PUT A FEW FLIERS IN MY BAG SOMEWHERE...

AH! HERE YA GO!

WONDERFUL! I'LL BE IN TOUCH!

YEAH, SHE'LL FIT IN *JUST FINE.*

OKAY, GANG! BRING IT *IN!* WE GOTTA GET *GOING!*

Y'KNOW--IT'S KIND OF FUNNY. I THOUGHT THAT PUSHING HAZEL AND MICHAEL AWAY WOULD KEEP THINGS THE SAME, AND I'D BE *HAPPY.*

BUT I WAS *MISERABLE!*

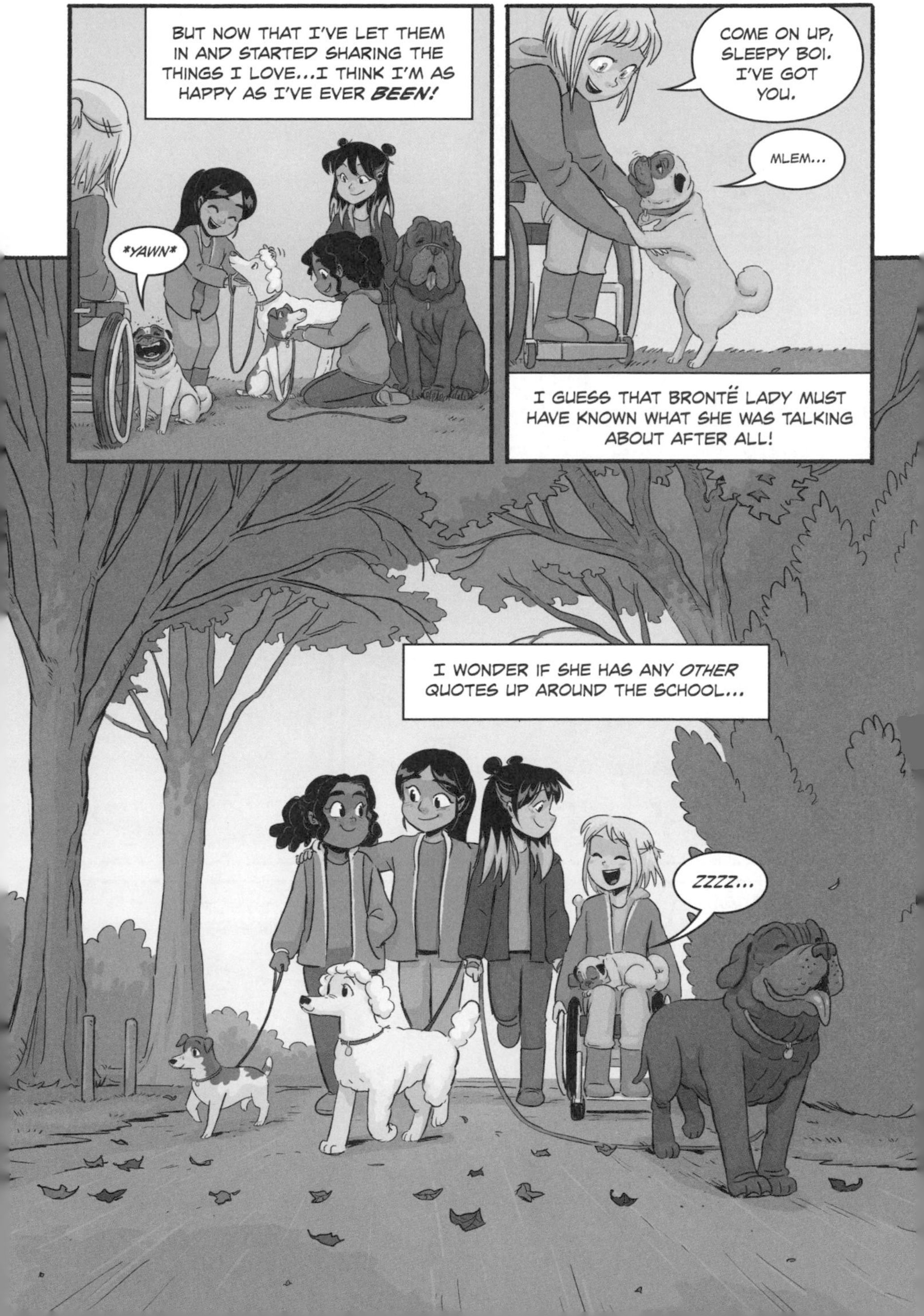
BUT NOW THAT I'VE LET THEM IN AND STARTED SHARING THE THINGS I LOVE...I THINK I'M AS HAPPY AS I'VE EVER *BEEN!*
YAWN
COME ON UP, SLEEPY BOI. I'VE GOT YOU.
MLEM...
I GUESS THAT BRONTË LADY MUST HAVE KNOWN WHAT SHE WAS TALKING ABOUT AFTER ALL!
I WONDER IF SHE HAS ANY *OTHER* QUOTES UP AROUND THE SCHOOL...
ZZZZ...

WHO'S GOT TWO THUMBS AND IS READY FOR *BBB?!*

THIS GIR--

OH... MICHAEL IS HERE.

HEY, BABE!

HEY, KIDDO! I JUST STOPPED BY TO SAY HI TO YOUR MOM.

SHE MENTIONED THAT IT WAS YOUR *BBB* NIGHT, SO I BROUGHT YOU A GIFT--

--IT'S A *BIG BEAN BAG!*

OH. THAT'S... ACTUALLY PRETTY COOL.

WELL, I KNOW I TAKE UP MORE THAN MY FAIR SHARE OF THE COUCH...

HAHA!

AND CONSIDER IT A TOKEN OF MY APPRECIATION FOR HOW WELL YOU GIRLS ARE TAKING CARE OF CHONK.

HE'S SO HAPPY THESE DAYS, AND I SWEAR HE'S EVEN LOST SOME *WEIGHT!*

REALLY?

WELL, NOT MUCH. MAYBE LIKE AN OUNCE? HAHA...*STILL!*

ANYWAY, I'LL GET OUT OF YOUR HAIR AND LET YOU LADIES HAVE YOUR NIGHT TOGETHER.

OKAY...THANKS SO MUCH FOR COMING OVER.

WHAT HAVE *YOU* GOT GOING ON TONIGHT?

OH, *BIG* PLANS. CHONK AND I HAVE A HOT DATE...

MAYBE WE'LL ORDER A *PIZZA!*

163

SIGH

HEY, MICHAEL--WHY DON'T YOU STAY AND HANG WITH US TONIGHT?

REALLY?!

A-ARE YOU *SURE?!*

I--I THOUGHT THIS WAS YOUR LADIES' NIGHT...

AH, WHATEVER.

BUT *YOU* HAVE TO PAY FOR THE BINGSU!

I...WELL I'D *LOVE* TO! WE CAN STOP AT MY PLACE ON THE WAY THERE AND FEED *CHONK!*

OH, THAT'S *GREAT!*

... JUST GOTTA GET THESE STUPID BOOTS OFF AGAIN ...

THANKS, BABE.

SHEESH, WHATEVER.

COME ON, MIKE. I'LL TEACH YOU HOW TO MAKE GAMJA BOKKEUM.

COOL!

YOU'RE CHOPPING THE ONIONS!

WELL, I GUESS THAT'S *IT!*

THE STORY OF HOW I ALMOST RUINED EVERYTHING, *BUT SOMEHOW DIDN'T!*

WELCOME TO
GROUSE MOUNTAIN

Grouse Grind

Baden Powell

MICHAEL IS STILL A DORK (OBVIOUSLY) BUT I ACTUALLY KINDA DON'T *MIND* HIM. HE LIKES TO SHARE HIS INTERESTS WITH US AND HE REALLY, REALLY SEEMS TO MAKE MY MOM *HAPPY.*

(THOUGH, PERSONALLY, I'M NOT SO CRAZY ABOUT ALL THIS *CLIMBING* OF THINGS.)

LOOKING BACK, I CAN SEE THAT I KINDA LOST MY WAY FOR A BIT.

AH!

TRIP!

WHOA!

MROW?

BUT WHAT CAN I SAY?

GOTCHA!

WHEN YOU FEEL THAT YOU DON'T *HAVE* MUCH, AND WHEN THE FEW THINGS YOU *DO* HAVE ARE SO *PRECIOUS* TO YOU, IT CAN BE SCARY TO THINK ABOUT LOSING THEM.

THANKS, MOM.

BUT *SHARING* ISN'T THE SAME AS *LOSING.* IF YOU CAN MAKE SPACE TO LET OTHERS IN...

...YOU'LL PROBABLY FIND THAT THERE'S SUDDENLY MORE ROOM FOR ALL *KINDS* OF THINGS.

COME ON, KIDDO! ALMOST *THERE!*

MORE ROOM FOR *FUN.*

MORE ROOM FOR *FRIENDSHIP.*

MORE *HAPPINESS.*

YOU GOOD?

YEAH...

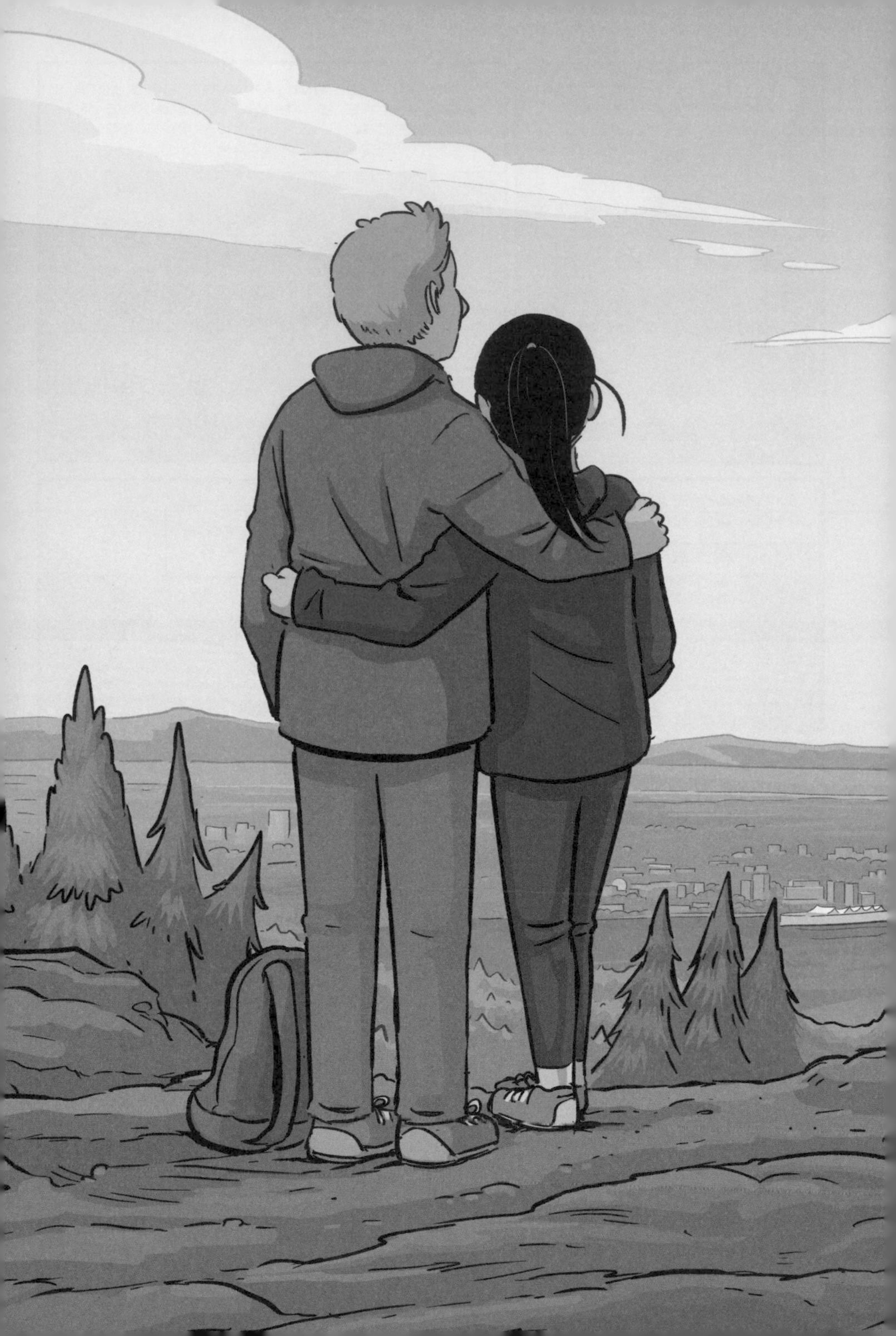

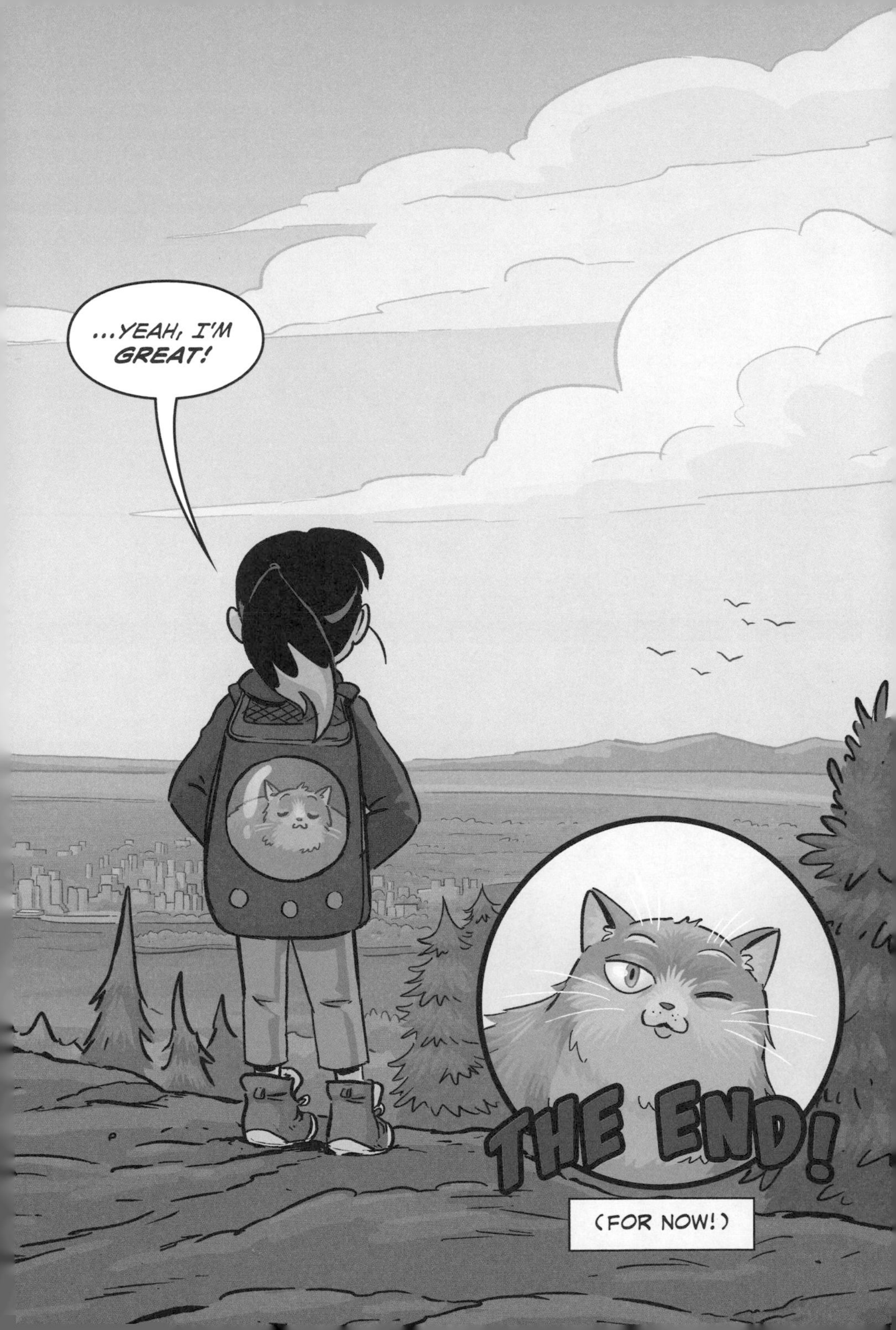
...YEAH, I'M GREAT!
THE END!
(FOR NOW!)

Acknowledgments

Mindy Makes Some Space was created while I was also busy making some space, as I worked on this book throughout my first pregnancy and the raising of my daughter, Kiki. I could not have done it without my amazing support system, and I'd like to give special thanks to these people for making work-life through motherhood a little easier.

Thank you to my brother/personal chef, Nicko; Adam, my forever cheerleader; Mama Gail, for being our family's anchor; and Nathan, the best work partner/friend an artist could ask for.

Thank you to our amazing team at Razorbill for all their hard work, especially Chris Hernandez, who believed in us and PAWS right from day one.

Thank you to our readers for the overwhelming support and love for *Gabby Gets It Together*. I hope you will love this one, too! —M. A.

———————————

Thanks to my wife, Rachel, for everything. Without her supporting my dreams and ambitions all these years, I never would have accomplished any of them.

Thanks to my friend and partner Michele, whose work on this series constantly impresses and inspires me. I'll be forever grateful to her for believing in and working with me to tell these stories. —N. F.

THE GIRLS OF

WILL RETURN!